WHEN LOVE COMES CALLING:

THE ULTIMATE LOVE

BIMPE GOLD-IDOWU

Published by The Seed Publishing House

Disclaimer

This is a work of fiction. Any names or characters, businesses or places, events or incidents are fictitious. Any resemblance to actual persons, living or dead, or actual events is purely coincidental.

Trigger Warning

This work has some scenes with family violence, verbal and physical abuse.

Books by Bimpe Gold-Idowu
Fiction - Print and Ebook
The Adamites: Protector of the Universe
Stare and Love Forever: A Contemporary Romance
When Love Coming: The Ultimate Love

Nonfiction – Religious books
Arts of Miracle
Overcoming Deceit: Expository on the World of Lies and Illusions

Other stories are on Kindle Vella
My Heart Prevails
The Heart Missed
Stare & Love Forever
The Adamites: Protector of the Universe Series 1
The Adamites: Alpha Series 2
When Love Comes Calling: The Ultimate Love
The Girl from the Sea: Richie and the Mermaid Princess Series 1

I dedicate this book to the Lord for His grace upon my life, and to all book lovers.

CHAPTER ONE

Jane carried her briefcase and made her way to the door of her well-furnished office. She yawned from her tedious day work.

"See ya on Monday Mirabel," she shouted towards her gentle-spirited, pretty secretary.

"See ya," Mirabel shouted back.

Jane remembered something, and she turned back to Mirabel.

"Are you still going on the weekend trip with that penniless guy?"

"Ouch! Jane." Mirabel frowned, sent a cold stare at Jane. "That's harsh, you know."

Jane Harply was a smart, intelligent and successful career young lady. In her mid-twenties; twenty-six. Jane believed that with money you can get whatever you want, without money, there is no reason to live. But her friend cum secretary, Mirabel, had the opposite nature of hers. Gentle and always going out of her way in helping others, even though she mostly gets hurt in the return of her good deeds, yet that did not deter her from seeking for the betterment of others.

"I'm pretty sure you are the one paying for that trip, Mira."

"Of course not, Jane. He may not be a millionaire, but he has a good job, and makes an honest living, plus he is a genuine believer."

"Hey, spare me that." Jane waved her hand in the air, visibly irritated. "Don't you know religion is just a scam?" She moved closer to Mirabel, placed her briefcase on the desk beside some piled up files Mirabel was working on. "My dad was a deacon in our church, always acting like a saint in front of the entire congregation, yet he was a monster at home."

"Not everyone is like your dad, Jane." Mirabel watched as Jane stared into space, her jaw clenched. A posture Mirabel knew too well and gave Jane's hand a gentle squeeze. Jane jolted back from her horrible past.

"Jane, there are good men out there and you can only see that if you give love a chance."

She jerked her hand away and stepped back. "Well, this is not about me, and don't give me that look. I hate to see it."

Mirabel sighed. She knew with Jane, there's no use talking about this matter. "I will keep praying for you."

"I don't need your prayer, am doing fine on my own."

"Anyway, I will see you on Monday," Mirabel resumed typing, but watched Jane from the corner of her eyes.

Jane understood Mirabel just dismissed her politely. She picked up her briefcase, adjusted her suit, and spoke once more to Mirabel. She wished Mirabel would stop being naïve and listen to her word of wisdom and learn from her experience, because this journey Mirabel called love is nothing but a journey of destruction. "So, you are determined to go with that guy?"

"Yep," Mirabel nodded without taking her attention away from the computer.

Jane gave a defeated sigh. "Well then, call me when you get back and be sure to always have that pepper spray with you every time, so the crook won't act funny."

"I told you he is a child of God," Mirabel reminded Jane. "Besides, we will not be getting intimate yet, not until our wedding night."

"And you believed that?" Jane rolled eyes up. "Mira, you are aware I came from what the church would call an ideal Christian home, having a deacon as a father and a deaconess as a mother. During my growing up, people always see my parents outside together, hosting different church events with my mom always singing my dad's praises. I remembered how my mother looked on the day she died or, better still, on the day my dad murdered my mom."

Before Mirabel could give her a response, Jane cuts in. "Anyway, see you later," she turned and left, unwilling to start another argument with the naïve Mirabel.

Jane Harply may be a beautiful lady on

the outside, with 5.7 feet tall, slim with a curvy hip, a long brown blonde hair, a semi-blue eye that looks like the surface of the ocean coupled with a small pointed noise. But, on the inside, Jane has always been a bitter female because of her childhood experiences.

***

"Hello miss," a voice jolted Jane back from her sad memory into the presence of an unfamiliar face in front of her.

"Yes?" she scowled at him; a habit she has grown accustomed to anytime she came in contact with the opposite gender. She gaze into the eyes of this muscular man standing in front of her and looking so authoritative.

"You are blocking the way." The man pointed to her back.

Her eyes followed his direction, surprised, realized she had been standing at the entrance of the mall's elevator. Jane remembered she has stopped to pick up some groceries she needed, only for her to get lost in her past reality.

"Oh... sorry." She muttered offhandedly and walked away from him.

"Are you alright, miss?" The man stepped beside her, trying to match her pace.

"Never mind," she shrugged her shoulder, trying to avoid his probing eyes.

"Joe Allen," he brought his hand forward for a handshake.

"What?" Jane asked, a bit confused.

"I am Joe Allen." He repeated as if he was addressing a ten-year-old slow child who could not grab a simple speech on time.

"Ooh! I'm Jane, Jane Harply," wondering why she even bothered replying his introduction. Well, she reminded herself, it was the right thing to do, at least courtesy demanded that from her.

Both of them moved into the mall, but Jane didn't want this conversation to continue, for she felt so uneasy with the presence of this strange man.

"Well, am going to that side. I guess you are going in the other direction." She said, even though she did not know which direction he's heading to.

"So, I will get going now," she discharged his unwanted company.

"Sure." He already sensed she didn't

want to be in his company any longer.

"See you later," he bade her leave and strode off in another direction. Just then, his phone rang. Joe picked up his call without giving another glance to Jane.

"Idiot," she swore under her breath. He didn't even ask for my number. Teeth grinding, Jane aimlessly dragged a cart without adding any groceries.

To Jane, all men were the same. Jane Harply believed all men want either sex or money from her, and to her, all men were worthless. In fact, she wanted nothing to do with them, especially marriage. She didn't want to end up dead like her mother, Susan.

***

"I told you to get back here now." Roared Desmond Harply. "Else, I will break your bones today, you, this worthless woman." Jane heard her father shouted at her mother.

"Leave me!" Susan screamed back at her husband. "Why do you keep doing this to me?"

Jane heard her mother, Susan, pleading with her dad. Jane tried to avert her head but could not and she tried to open her eyes from her nightmare. Engulfed by the scene in her dream, she saw herself when she was a ten-year-old child, standing in the middle of their big sitting room holding the tip of her blue dress with her two hands, visibly shaking by the scene taken place in front of her and unable to move or run from the brutal sight. Jane wanted to block those horrible noises from her ears. She wanted to scream or make any sound to stop these abuses toward her helpless mother, and suddenly her surroundings turned dark. She tried to focus on her surroundings, moved towards the kitchen door, reflecting some light. At her front, laying on the cold kitchen floor, was her mother, Susan, with blood dripping down from her head.

Jane woke up from her nightmare with a throbbing headache. Not again. She held her head with both hands. She has done everything possible to stop these recurring nightmares from destroying her state of mind and sleep, but nothing worked.

CHAPTER TWO

Jane rushed out of the bathroom to pick her call. It was Mirabel on the other side. Jane pouted her lips. "Yes, why are you calling me by this time?"

"Are you still mad at me"?"

"Mira, I'm not angry with you, but I don't want you to experience the same pain my mother did."

"My man is different, Jane. Besides, Pastor Ben approves our relationship. The church has added us to the list of couples in waiting."

"That is more reason for you to break away from this relationship. It was the pastor that killed my mom..."

"You told me it was your dad, now you

said the pastor." Mirabel cuts in.

"That's because you do not know the full story."

Mirabel sighed. "Fine, Jane. I want to hear the full story. Tell me what really happened."

"I think you need to know because I don't want you to be another victim." Jane switched the voice call to video, placed the phone on her small adjustable table she just bought and sat down on the rug. "It was on a Friday night. We just returned from the Bible study. We attended Holy Saints Assembly Church. My dad was a deacon in the church while my mother was a deaconess and a Sunday school teacher. My parents always look like happy couple to outsiders. Mom always dressed me up in beautiful bright colored dresses, which made many children in my Sunday school class did envy me. Apart from dad been a church deacon, he was also the church's patron." Jane had a sad smile on her face. "Desmond Harply was a very rich man. He was in charge of a fifty-two-year-old family business. He inherited one of the largest pharmaceutical companies in the States. So, the church felt blessed to have such an important personality in their midst, according to word of the head pastor, Pastor James Smith. In the eyes of the pastor, my father could do no wrong, even when mom reported dad to him. Pastor James quickly ushered us into his office for the fear of another member hearing mom complained about the church patron." Jane stood up to take a cold drink from the refrigerator. She opened the drink and gulped it down her throat, threw the can into the dustbin, then took another drink out with a chocolate cake before returning to her call with Mirabel. Her friend watched her in silence, feeling consigned, but kept a straight face.

"Do you want to stop, Jane?"

"Why? Are you scared to find out your Raymond is another Desmond Harply?"

"It's okay, Jane," Mirabel raised her hands to stop Jane's malicious attack. "Please go on."

"Pastor James pointed out the words in the vow my parents made on the day of their wedding; for better and for worse, till death do them part. And truly, Mirabel, the death of my mom, parted them."

"I'm sorry, Jane."

Jane grabbed a book she placed beside her pillow and flung it away. "Don't!"

"I take it back, and calm down, please. You know I don't mean it that way." Mirabel felt helpless watching Jane in such a state.

"I remembered sitting on the chair beside my mom on that day. Mom went to Pastor James to report the physical and verbal abuses from dad. But guess what? Pastor James countered these allegations with the same words in the Bible."

Mirabel gasped. "How could he do that?"

"Pastor James instructed mom to be submissive in all situations, as divorce goes against Christian teachings. He said that he couldn't hold father responsible for his actions because he had a premonition of the devil attempting to provoke them. Even, he can see the devil wants to use mom to break her own home." Jane gaze into space and she went back to Pastor James' office.

"Have you ever seen a perfect home or man before?" Pastor James asked Susan.

"No," Susan shook her head. "But..."

"Mrs. Harply," Pastor James held a finger up. "I understand your predicament, and I promise to speak with your husband. Many women are praying for a husband like yours, just so you know. Do you know what the Bible says about woman and home in Proverbs 14:1?" Giving her a sharp, penetrating gaze. Pastor James is a man who likes to quote every law in the Bible, and he expects everyone to obey, especially the women of faith. "The Bible says a wise woman will build up her home, but a foolish woman will destroy her home." He smiled at Susan, but his eyes demanded total obedience from her. "Mrs. Harply, don't allow the devil to use you to destroy your house. Let's pray."

Seeing Jane lost in thought, Mirabel yelled her name. "Jane!"

"What? Oh sorry, Mirabel." Jane popped open the can of drink and took a sip before she continued. "On getting home that fateful Friday, dad turned on mom with a thunderous slap on her left cheek. I watched mom landed on the floor with a bewildered

look on her angel-like face, still she ordered
me to go to her room. I couldn't move my feet
because I was so startled by the sound that
my body was shaking. Dad dragged my mom
by her hand towards their room. Mom was
on the floor, begging him to let her go. I
guess she realized her plea was fruitless.
Mom jerked her hand away from his hold
and ran into the kitchen. Before she could
close the kitchen's door, dad kicked the door
opened with his left foot. He grabbed mom
and landed another slap on her face, then
threw her on the floor." Jane went back to
that scene.

"I told you to come back, but you ran
away. How dare you report me to the pastor?"
Desmond's eyes blazing with terror. "What
will the pastor do?" He laughed, took out a
comb from his trouser's pocket, and combed
his curls. He returned the comb to his
trouser's pocket. "Your pastor is only
interested in my money, and I will keep
donating a large amount for the church, so
God will always overlook my wrongdoing.
After all, am a cheerful giver." He wet his
lower lip. He landed another kick on her

stomach. Susan gasped and wriggled her body in pain.

From Jane's standing spot in the living room, she could see her father assaulting her mum with blood dripping down her mum's head. She saw her mum on the floor looking so weak and her father laughing like someone who has lost it. But what she saw next was the most horrible thing she had ever witnessed.

Jane went quiet, closed her eyes, then opened it. She turned her gaze to Mirabel with a sly smile. "Three months after mom's death, I was standing at the witnessed box in the court, narrating what I saw on that Friday night. On that day, Mira, I vowed never to forgive my dad or believe a word coming out of the church's altar. I'm going to church because I enjoy the singing, but my going would only be because of the joy and solace I find in the chorus. For the preaching of the pastors, she will never let that get to her."

"What happened after that?"

"The judge sentenced dad to life imprisonment, and I went to my uncle's home. Everything was going fine till Uncle Harry and his family died in a plan crash. I was alive thanks to the flu I developed, and the doctor advised I stayed back and not to travel, so my health will not worsen. This saved me from crashing with the family, but turned me into an orphan again. Pastor James came forward to request for my custody. Since there were no other relatives to take me in, my custody of went to him. This began another horrible channel in my life."

"You are scaring me Jane, what could be worse than what you have passed through?"

"Pastor James was a pervert, Mirabel. He would come into my room in the night while his wife was asleep and physical abused me, then he would clean me up and forced me to take the liquid drink he always brought along whenever he came to abuse me. When I could not take it anymore, I ran away from the mission house where Pastor James and his family lived. I had to sleep at the bus station for three days before the Children's Bureau officers found her. This time I was ready to die, so I fought back against going to Pastor James' house, told them how he had been drugging his wife just to come and abuse me at night. They got Pastor James Smith arrested and charged him for sexual abuse of a minor with three other offences. The jury found him guilty of all charges and the judge sentenced him to 17 years' imprisonment."

Mirabel couldn't control her tears anymore. Jane saw her face and frowned.

"But Jane..." before Mirabel could complete her sentence, Jane ended the call, switched off her bedroom light and lay on the bed.

Though part of that day will always stay locked away in her memory because it's too shameful to narrate. She loved her mother too much to reveal that part. Jane closed her eyes and doze off.

Jane switched on the light and glanced at the small clock by her bedside. It was 5:10 am. Today was a Saturday. She had nothing much to do in the morning, not until the afternoon she would go to the club, she reminded herself. Jane recently joined a volunteers club protecting the rights of women and abused teenagers. She joined this group because of what she went through while growing up.

Jane had to go to a foster home. It was there she met Mirabel, and they both became friends. The difference between these two friends was faith. Mirabel believed in God and His undiluted love for humankind, while Jane acknowledge the existence of God, but believed that God is too faraway to be bothered with her. Jane Harply believed God is partial and she will live her life the way she wanted without getting herself involved in anything that consigned God.

CHAPTER THREE

"**H**i miss, we meet again." Jane turned to see the person with the familiar masculine voice.

"You?"

"Yes, me," Joe beamed a smile at her. "What are you doing here?"

"What?" She raised her chin. "I should be the one asking you that because I'm part of this club," she glared at him with her left arm around her waist.

"Really?" His eyes lightened up.

"Being a lawyer, I volunteered to be the club's legal counsel."

"That's great, am impressed. I'm glad we'll be working together."

"What! Are you a lawyer also?"

"Oh no," Joe shook his head slowly, seen her confusion, he ruffled his hair. "Well, am into entertainment."

"Entertainment as a job?" she frowned, not sure of what he meant.

"Yeah, am into film directing... though, I act sometimes."

"I see," Jane dimmed her eyes, unable to see the correlation between acting and helping woman and teenagers out from their miseries. She chuckled, tried not to show her confusion. "You are an actor, uh... movie director, right?"

"Yeah," He nodded.

"And you are volunteering to act or entertain the club members?"

"Oh my, oh my," his eyebrows raised, he studied her rigid posture. "You probably think actors are some flippant characters. Well, apart from showbiz, am also a life coach, counselor and an author."

"That's much better," she remarked, not bothering to hide her relief. "At least you still have something decent you are doing to put food on your table." She stopped to fully assessed him, gazing at him from head to toe.

He looks really handsome, she thought to herself. "What genres do you write?"

"Christian fiction and nonfiction," surprised at her question.

"And films?" Hoping to hear something interesting.

"Same thing... films that teach biblical principles."

"Are you for real?" A bewildered look on her face.

"Pardon?" Joe looked confused at her.

"You said you are into Christian books and films?"

"Yes?" Unsure what she was driving at.

Do you really think you can make a living or become a star with your religious content?"

"Riches and glory are from the Lord."

"It makes sense to me now," she shook her head and moved nearer to him.

"You are one of those church people."

"Sorry?"

"I said you are one of those fanatics who expects God to physically come down from heaven and make things better just for them."

Joe stared at her in shock. He didn't

expect her to sound so condescending.

"Are you not a Christian?" Joe pointed to her hand band which had the inscription of her church's logo, Christ Peace Assembly on it.

Jane followed the direction of his glance. She lifted her hand. "Of course, I am a Christian, but that doesn't mean I believe the jargon your pastors preach." She narrowed her eyes. "I'm too intelligent for those lies."

Joe did not know what to make of this. He looked sad and uneasy. "You are a Christian, but you do not believe the words of pastors?"

She moved closer to look directly into his eyes. "Those words in the Bible they claimed to be from God were just words by other fellows like you and I. They wrote what their audience will love to read," she felt mesmerized by his brown eyes. "They were authors just like you." She changed her handbag from her left hand to the right, probably to ease the tension in her left hand, and moved back. "Or you want to tell me God also speaks to you?"

"Of course, yes." Joe didn't like her manners. "Through His word, the Holy Bible."

"Really?" she raised her eyebrows.

"Men wrote the Bible as you said, but it was through the inspiration of the Holy Spirit." He felt helpless.

"How did you confirm that?" Her probing eyes held him captive.

Joe lifted his right hand to his head, looking very distressed. Joe knew he felt attracted to this woman who has a look of an angel. He even saw her in his dream yesterday, playing a Scrabble game under a red umbrella while their three kids; two looking identical boys and a girl that has the same blonde hair with this woman building sand castle together. In his dream, they looked like one happy family. The dream convinced him God was telling him something about his future plan. But now, this woman doesn't sound like someone that can ever be on God's agenda, Joe thought miserably within himself. Looking lost and heartbroken, he tried to find the right word to convince Jane.

A cheerful chubby middle-aged Caroline

walked towards them, gasping for breath. "Hey guys." She looked like she had been running.

"Sorry guys, am late," she's a co-founder of the club.

"Oh no," Joe gave her a smile, but she could see he looked troubled. "Many are yet to arrive."

"Good." She looked relieved to hear that. Caroline inhaled some fresh air. "You should have seen how I was hurrying to be here before the action starts." Caroline looked from one to the other. She sensed there's more to their presence there which she had interrupted. "I see you guys have met."

"Yea... yeah," His voice sounded too hoarse for his liking. "Though we have met prior to today."

"Really?" curious Caroline looked from one to another, debating if it would be a good idea to probe more. She shrugged off the urge. "That's better," she simply said. It's not her place to dabble in their privacy, Caroline reminded herself.

"Well, it was just a brief encounter,"

Jane blurted. "Not that we are friends or anything like that," Jane added, determined to clear the air. She didn't want any misunderstanding, especially when he's part of the church that killed her mother.

"May we head inside now?" Caroline suggested, trying to ease the tension.

"I think we should go start the meeting. Others will join us as they come in." Caroline can see the uneasiness on Joe's face.

"Alright," they both agreed

Joe Allen was a man in his late twenties, tall and muscular in physics, with a dark skin and brown eyes. He had the look of those male models women would love to see on the cover of a clothing magazine. Joe Allen migrated from North Ireland with his mother when he was just six years old.

Joe remembered asking his mother why the police had led his father away that day at the court.

"The judge said your father embezzled the money of his clothing line and sent him to jail for seven years, son"

Confused, little Joe stared at his mother's tear-stained face but got no answer.

"My husband is not a thief." Joe heard his mother kept repeating.

Three years later, Joe's uncle gave him the good new. "Joe, boy, do you remember your father's friend, Lucas Bright?"

Joe went still. "Is he coming to arrest mom now? He called my dad a thief, and the cops came to send him to jail. The clothes belonged to dad, but that wicked man said dad stole it."

"Lol," scratching his chin, he tried to look for ways to explain the situation to this young and innocent boy. "Let's me start this way. Lucas' wife went to the authority to confess for her husband's wrongdoing. The doctors have diagnosed Lucas with skin cancer and already in his last days. It was a well-planned game to set up his friend for embezzlement so he alone could own the company. Because of her confession, Stephen, your father, will leave the prison and come over to America to be with you and your mom. My boy, your dad went to prison for a purpose. "

"What purpose?"

"Your dad has met with the message of

the gospel and has embraced a new way of life. Preaching is the path Stephen opted for. This his new way was an answered prayer of Linda, Joe's mother."

Joe didn't understand a prayer that will send someone to prison.

"Come sit beside me, son. I will tell you a brief story about your parents."

Joe went to sit beside his uncle. He loved listening story and his uncle was good at it.

"Linda, your mom, was a good girl from a Christian home and very committed to her faith, but Stephen, your dad, was of a free spirit. He sometimes laughed at Linda for always been too serious and holy to enjoy life to the fullest. Stephen knew Linda did not approve of his friendship with Lucas. To Linda, Lucas was too cunning for her liking, but Stephen thought she was exaggerating. Stephen and Lucas Bright met during their first year in college, they both studied Business Administration, but Lucas dropped out of college when he met a man who offered him a partnership in an oil business, not knowing he was into an illegal bunkering in faraway Africa. After a raid by the local authority, federal security arrested them and he spent several months in a correctional center. The judge freed him for lack of evidence connecting him to the organization. He signed no partnership contract with Daniel; Lucas went with him to Africa with only a word of mouth." He checked to see if young Joe understood what he was saying. Joe gave him a nod. "You may be too young to remember, but after your dad graduated from college, he went to enroll at a fashion designing school, and your mom became a teacher. A month after his graduation from fashion school, they got married at the back of Linda's parents' garden, with only close family and friends in attendance. Some weeks after their marriage, Stephen met Lucas at a grocery store and he invited Lucas home. After their meeting, both set up a clothing line together. A decision Linda was against, but Stephen just waved it off. I'm sure he later regretted his decision."

"But my dad was trying to help him. Mrs. Rachael told us on Sunday to always help our friends."

Uncle Roy chuckled. "Yes, my boy, your

Sunday school teacher is right. Bad people like Lucas shouldn't stop you from being good. Anyway, that was in the past. Your dad is coming to America, and I have enrolled in Adoration Theology College. He told me he wants to study Religious Studies and am glad your mom is doing well in her clothing line."

Nine days after Stephen Allen graduated from the seminary on a Sunday morning at 5:24am, Linda gave birth to a baby girl and they named her Jessica, for she was a consolidation gift from God after everything they had been through.

Joe, growing up in the church, has had his share of battles. Even though his parents were active believers in the church, yet they faced many antagonisms from some church pastors and influential members in the church. Young Joe was the one that felt most of those brutal attacks since these people could not face his parents, so they take it out on him.

When his parents could not endure the toxic attitudes from the co-pastors any longer, Stephen and Linda Allen left to start Haven

Christian Fellowship, a fellowship they started in their home with just twelve members, including their family. It was a small gathering, but they were happy to be working for God now without facing opposition and the unhealthy rivalry from the so-called ministers of God. Within the space of five months, their members miraculously grew and their garden could no longer accommodate the congregation. Members also demanded for more spiritual programs, especially Sunday service, and this will not be possible in their back garden. With the help of two members and the money Linda raised from her clothing line, they secured a small building for their ministry. They changed the name of their fellowship to Haven Christian Church and registered it as a church with some church members as trustees. The family and church grew from strength to strength.

Joe looked back at his twenty-nine years of existence, from his childhood, high school day, to his university level. He has God to be grateful for. His life has been smooth so far, not until recently when he is trying to make something out of his career.

Stephen and Linda Allen wanted Joe to toil their ministerial path and take up the pastoral calling since Joe was the first son of the family, but Joe wanted to do something else. He only wanted to be in the film industry. To him, pastoral work was too tiring and time-consuming and he did not want to take up the responsibility of carrying other people's cross. Most will not even appreciate your efforts and later rebel against you. Joe Allen had witnessed some church members his parents had helped, for them to badmouth his parents, always pointing out his parents' negative sides and never praising their positive efforts. Joe wanted nothing to do with the toxic attitudes of ungrateful members. It's a pity, these kinds of people take up most percentage of church congregation. Joe thought to himself.

"Help me Lord," Joe whispered. He has been praying a lot. Joe prayed for a change in his career. Everyone he came in contact with always praise his directing skills yet, he did not know why he kept getting dropped, except to get acting roles not over one to two scenes into the film production, Joe wondered what he needed to do to change his stars, and now he could not keep the picture of this strange angry woman out of his subconsciousness.

But why so much bitterness in her? Joe wondered.

He let his eyes wandered to where Jane was sitting, some two rows away from him. He wondered again how such a beauty could have such bitterness toward God's ministers. What could be her reason? Joe intended to find out. Perhaps he will understand her views, Joe consoled himself.

At exactly 4:45pm, the meeting ended. Joe quickly moved up to Jane. She was gathering up some papers that fell out of her handbag. Joe bent down to help with it and his eyes glanced through the paper as he picked them up.

"What!" He exclaimed, looking up at Jane with disapproval.

"These are church lyrics," he accused Jane. To Joe, going to the church was not bad. In fact, it signified she was not entirely a lost soul, only a wounded one, but saying the word of the gospel in vain, that was going extreme.

"Yes, so?" She replied with a frown, snatching the scripts from his hand as if she was a hen whom he just attacked her little chicken.

"And what are you doing with those?"

"I'm a chorister in our church," Jane responded curtly.

"Are you kidding me?" Joe queried. He shook his head in disbelieved.

"You may think whatever you want," she muttered, unperturbed with a shrug. "I am one of the best in the choir," a sly smile on her face.

"Oh, men," Joe teased her. "I will love to see that," he added as Jane was packing the scripts into her bag. She felt uneasy with him, and her throat felt as if she swallowed an enormous cooked egg which refused to go down her belly.

"You can tag along if you wish," she blurted out before realizing what she had done. "Well... I know you are probably too busy for such frivolous stuff," she quickly added, trying to find an excuse to deter him from going with her.

"I'll love to come," Joe looked amused. He ignored her last remark.

Jane castigated herself for what she has just done. She wanted to send this irritating man away, but with this invitation, Jane believed she had just given him another chance to ruffle her calm composure. She grumbled in annoyance to herself.

Joe was super excited to receive an invitation from Jane, either she was willing or not.

Perhaps this is the Lord's doing. Joe told himself.

CHAPTER FOUR

"**H**ello Jane," Sandra, the assistant choir coordinator, greeted Jane in her usual cheerful manner. Sighting Joe, she nodded to Jane while she stole a curious glance at Joe. "He's with you?"

"Of course, he's with me. Why else would he be here?" Jane looked towards Joe, standing with a calm expression, observing the church setting.

"Joe, this is Sandra. Sandra, this is Joe."

"Hello Joe," beaming a seductive look at Joe. She offered her hand to Joe for a handshake.

"Hi Sandra," Joe politely accepted her handshake.

Sandra turned to Jane with a naughty

grimace. "Nice to see Jane with a handsome guy today."

"Hey," Jane glared at Sandra.

"I'm glad I came," Joe responded, not bothered by Jane's frown.

"You may sit over there." Jane motioned him to the pews some meters away from the choir barricade.

"Sure," Joe gave her a nod and moved towards the pews to take a sit.

"Hi," some new choristers entering the sanctuary echoed.

"Hi," the blonde, average height and chubby Tina waved at Joe

"We have a company today," Dan the Choir Coordinator asked curiously. He gave Jane a wink.

"Do we have to wait for others to arrive?" Trying to hide her embarrassment.

Tina left their circle and went to sit beside Joe on the pew. "Are you a new convert here?" Batting her eyelids.

Joe flashed her his knock out smile. "Maybe... if she will let me," he gave a nod towards Jane.

"Ooh oh mine," Daisie, one chorister,

teased Jane.

"Well, you don't need her permission, handsome... I am giving you mine outrightly," Tina uttered, rolling her eye up seductively.

"Hey... do you mind getting over here and let's start with our rehearsal?" Jane hollered at Tina, visibly irritated. What a flirt. Jane foamed within herself. Imagine such behavior in the house of God. "Rubbish," she mumbled angrily.

"What?" asked the curious Sandra. She poked Jane lightly by her side.

"Oh, sorry," Jane realized she had said that out loud.

Jane stole a glance at Joe. His handsome features were undeniable. Gazing at him alone makes her blood race. She could hear her heart beating loudly, threatening to break out of her slim body. Jane glanced around the faces near her, silently hoped no one was hearing the loud pounding of her heartbeat.

In the past, Jane had tried to have a meaningful relationship. She once considered marriage with her last boyfriend Harry, but it turned out to be messy with verbal abuses hauled at each other. Jane knew she had some part to play in the messy relationship, but most of her silly boyfriends caused the larger issues. She believed all men were pretenders. To make the matter worse, none of her unfortunate boyfriends were as buoyant as she was.

Jane Harply high financial status did not just come from her hard work or career, she was a millionaire from birth. Her monster of a father inherited a multi-million even if not called 'multi-billion' dollar pharmaceutical company, which the mantle passed down to Jane been the only heir to the long family company. Jane wanted nothing to do with her father. She vowed never to associate with her father and she has no interest in running his legacy. Upon Jane's graduation at the college, her father's attorneys requested her to take charge of her father's empire along with their mini-estate. Jane declined all, but since her father would be ever stuck in prison for the rest of his life, he had all his wealth handed over to her. After much persuasion, Jane accepted the assets. After all, her mother was just as eligible for half of her father's wealth as he was. Upon acquiring all, Jane sold the estate and donated seventy percent of the money received to several charitable foundations. She then handed over the ownership of the company to the executives. Jane told them to look for another person to run the company and never to bother her with the company issues. She made it known that she cared not if the company fails or not. She wanted to forget everything about her father. Still, a large sum of different currencies, either direct deposits, wire transfers or checks, always find their ways into her bank account, which she usually gave out generously to the needy. The more she gave out, Jane realized it kept coming back.

Some other choristers made their way into the sanctuary. Several arrived some minutes late after they have started their weekly practice for the Sunday thanksgiving service. Joe watched the choir performed and got deeply captivated when Jane took up the lead. Jane has a soprano voice, and she sang in such an angelic way. Her face lit up when she sang and Joe felt at peace just watching her sing. He could see how she looked so different when singing. Her icy edge seemed to dissolve. She looked so happy and innocent. Joe wondered why Jane had such a sad and kind of lonely face whenever she seemed to stare into the space. That's a thing he must find out. He told himself.

The lyrics of the hymnal the choir sang were inspirational, combined with Jane's soothing voice when she pronounced the words.

Her beautiful voice filled the air as she sang "O'hour of pray..." and the rest followed.

Joe Allen bowed down his head, his hands folded and eyes closed. He prayed to God.

"Thank you, Lord, for leading me to her. I can feel there's a deep wound in her, but I promise to help heal it with your words, love, and patience. I will bring her to you, Abba, father."

***

"By the power given to me, I pronounce you husband and wife. Now you may kiss your bride," the officiating priest declared Joe and Jane as a couple in front of over three hundred guests who came to grace their wedding. The guests cheered them with claps and Jane's flower girls rained roses and mixed colored berries on the couple. Joe stood tall in his black tuxedo with a red bow tie. He looked up and whispered his appreciation to God, but Jane just stood still with a dull expression. Within her, there was turmoil running into chaos, trying to dampen her new found joy. It was supposed to be a day of joy, but with her mother's predicament, she looked at Joe with a confused expression. Jane hoped she would not end up six feet under like her mother. Anyway, that was the main reason she learned martial art, she thought. She could always defend herself should she ever needed to.

"Hello!" Raymond shouted at the top of his voice for attention, and all gathered around him. Raymond was Joe's childhood friend, co-incidentally, he was the same penniless guy Mirabel, Jane's secretary and best friend, had fallen in love with. Both had gotten married eight months ago, and Mirabel was now heavily pregnant. Despite her heavy pregnancy, Jane had insisted she wanted Mirabel as her chief bridesmaid. Her two other bridesmaids were Sandra, her assistant choir coordinator, and Tina, her annoying church friend.

"I have a special song for my buddy Joe and his queen." Raymond told the happy gathering. The younger generations gave loud cheers. Joe drew Jane closer to him in an embrace and plastered a kiss on her neck. He could sense the fear and uncertainty building up in her mind, but he was determined to fill her life with so much joy that she would forget the misery of her childhood.

***

"Cuts!" Joe barked at the actors.

He stood up from where he sat at the back of the camera crew and moved to the casts, who were misinterpreting their roles with a conflicting expression on their faces.

"You guys are supposed to be bosom friends." Joe stood up from his seat and moved in between the two middle-aged men.

"He is confiding in you." Talking to the Chinese man on the left. "Your expression ought to be calm, with your head slightly lifted to the front and your ear turned a bit towards him." Joe moved away. "Again," he ordered.

"Stop!" the producer barked an order as he came into the studio with three other men. He turned to Joe with a thunderous look.

"The company has fired you!" He spat.

"Pardon?" Joe asked in shock, having a hard time dejecting what the producer just said.

"I said we fired you," the producer grunted.

"Mr. Aries.... w... why?" Joe stammered. He suddenly felt nauseated, at the same time his eyes were going blurry. He could feel his ear ringing and his head hammered with severe pain. Joe sweated profusely. He had to support himself with the camera stand. Just when he thought he had finally made it, this happened.

"You can't do that," Joe protested faintly to the producer.

"Says who?" the producer dared Joe with a thunderous look. He turned to the man beside him. "Over to you, Director Wayne," he gave a nod to the man in the blue suit.

"Alright boss," Director Wayne bowed to him.

He turned to Joe again. "You will receive your paycheck in the next one hour, you can leave now," he dismissed Joe.

***

Joe left with a heavy heart as he tried to find his way to the bus station. Jane has tried to get Joe a Porsche car, but he declined. Joe insisted he wanted to buy his first car with his hard-earned money, and his first car was going to be Porsche; a car worth several dollars. Joe got to the bus station and sat down on the bench there, lost in thought. His thought went back to several jobs he had applied for, from directing job to acting. In all auditions, he always got rejected in the last minutes.

The acting role he got last was the worst. They dismissed him without a pay. The director had accused him of spreading flu to the lead actress even though Joe himself had no flu. It was a single moment Joe sneezed because the lead actress sprayed a perfume directly into Joe's face. Instead of her to apologize, she glared at Joe when he sneezed and she stormed off the set. Joe Allen's termination came ten minutes later. Joe bowed down his head, wrapping his hands round his body. He cried bitterly.

CHAPTER FIVE

It was late in the night when Joe finally made his way home. He got home by 10:56pm to meet the worried-looking Jane.

"Where have you been?" she attacked him with a query, looking so worried.

"They fired me," Joe simply responded. He could not bring himself to look at Jane in the eyes.

"What? Again?" Jane asked with her eyes wide opened. Joe burst into fresh tears with his body trembling.

"Oh, my," looking at Joe sobbing profusely, and his body trembled. She felt sorry for him. Joe looked like a three-year-old boy who lost his candy.

"Come over here," she drew him closer to

herself in a tight hug. Jane patted him on the back and consoled him. "It's okay, love, don't cry."

"It's not okay," he replied between sob. Jane used her right hand to lift Joe's chin up.

She looked into his eyes. "It's okay really, I got you a directing contract with a multimillion-dollar adult film production company."

"What!" Joe exclaimed.

"Yeah, a contract with a multimillion-dollar film production company," Jane responded with a smile.

Joe looked confused. "But you mention something in between."

"As in?" Trying to rack her brain for what was missing.

"Well, what's important is the pay, dearie. It's your dream job with a lot of zeros." She flashed him a smile, looking thrilled.

Joe simply looked at her. He failed to understand why this did not seem like good news to him. He felt so uneasy.

"Where is the written contract?" he asked Jane.

"There." She pointed to the letter placed

on the center table in their modest living room. "Hold on, let me get it for you."

Jane could sense Joe's icy feelings. He did not seem ecstatic about this news. She hoped there would not be any issue to it.

Joe opened a big brown envelope and brought out the contents. Jane kept smiling while he read through. Slowly his expression changed, from shocked to sad to angry.

He looked up angrily at Jane. "Do you know the type of rubbish job this is?"

"What rubbish job?" She replied with a defense look.

"It's an adult film production company," he fired at her, trying to suppress the rage building up within him.

"So?" Jane shrugged her shoulder.

"You expect me to direct an adult content movie?" He asked again, as if she lacked the understanding of what an adult film entails.

"And what is the problem with that?"

Joe stood up from the chair, went to the kitchen to pour himself a glass of water. He sipped the water, let out a long breath, and went back to the living room.

He took a stool and positioned it opposite Jane. Joe looked directly into her eyes and said to her. "You want me to direct a movie where two or more people will have a live direct sex, two unmarried people?" He emphasized.

"You are only going to direct them, not have sex yourself." Jane countered. "Plus, the money is so good... you can use the money to start up your own company." She quickly added.

Joe looked at her in amazement. He could not believe his ears.

"I am going to tear these up now."

"Don't you dare!" she yelled at him with so much heat, her eyes blazing. "At this junction, leave your principles and religious nonsense. All this while we have been living off my money and I never complained. It's time you live up to my expectations and be the man.... you can't continue claiming holy while you insist on staying in the film industry," she castigated Joe.

"I gave you a decent job at my dad's company even though I vowed never to go there again, but because of you I compromised, yet you rejected the job," she accused him.

Joe tried to defend himself, but she held up her finger to shut him up. "Today, you listened while I talk." She commanded. "Yes, I married you because I saw you as a man of principles. I believed you to be differed from my dad, but what did you give me in return, poverty and a boring life? Despite many jobs out there today, still you choose to be in the film industry, but you refused to do anything against your principles. That is the main reason they always fire you. Now I got you a mouth-watering deal and you want to reject this? Fine, what do you want to do?" She asked, looking heartbroken with tears in her eyes.

"I'm going to the seminary," he replied soberly.

Jane's eyes widen, she could not register what he just said into her brain.

"Pardon?" she asked again to be sure she heard right.

"I am going to the seminary."

"Are you nut?" Jane asked, looking bewildered. Joe swallowed hard, took a deep breath, and said, "God told me today to go to the seminary."

"And you expect me to believe that jargon?" She shook her head in disbelief.

He sighed heavily. "I have known for sometime, but I was asking for grace to postpone it for later in the future, I wanted to make a name for myself in the film industry first... but I guess the Lord is not having any of that, he wants a better plan for me."

Jane stared hard at him. "And when did you realize this nonsense?"

"For sometime now, but I got confirmation today at the bus-station."

"So, what do you want to do now?" She asked, running her fingers through her hair.

"I will leave for the seminary in three weeks' time and I will be there for three and half years," he informed Jane, feeling sorry for the steps he had to take.

Jane tried to stay strong. "You will leave me alone here in three weeks' time to go to some goddammit school for an entire three and half years and you want me to stay put in this place waiting for you to come back like a docile illiterate wife?" She berated him. Jane sat on the rug with tears flowing freely from her eyes.

"I thought you would be different, but you turned out just as selfish as my father."

"Don't you dare compare me with that monster," he threatened.

"But you are no different." She fired back. Jane used her palm to wipe off her tears, stood up and declared.

"Now listen carefully, Mr. Joe Allen. You have two options: stay home, accept the job, and continue our marriage, or leave for your seminary in pursuit of a false deity, ending our marriage."

"What! You can't do that," he protested, standing up to meet her gaze.

"If you leave for that seminary, then we will be officially over."

"Please Jane," Joe went on his knees. "Don't do this to me." He tried to hold Jane's hand, but she stopped him.

"You know I truly love you, Jane. I really do with my whole heart," Joe pleaded, sobbing afresh. He looked terrified.

"Try to understand, please. I can't do

this without your support. I need you in my life, darling." His emotional pleas had no effect on Jane.

She refused to move one bit, and all she could see was her childhood church, her dad smiling while addressing the congregation. Jane tried to block this memory. It hurt her head remembering these sad occurrences. Jane tried to stay focused on the present matter. She shut her eyes and saw the evil face of Pastor Desmond trying to force himself on her.

"I have made my decision, if you decide to join yourself with those that have hurt me terribly in the past. Then I have no choice but to divorce you, but till then, you have three weeks to think about this and decide if you want to stay with me or aligned yourself with my enemies. I never vowed to marry a pastor. I married a simple actor and maybe a mere church member, but definitely not a pastor." Jane replied coldly.

"You can sleep in the guest room." She added and headed to the bedroom, leaving Joe on his knees in the living room.

***

"Leave me please," Jane heard her mother's voice pleading. She started running from one room to the other in their magnificent house.

"Mummy, where are you" Jane called out, searching furiously for her mother. In an instant, she changed into her childhood appearance and was standing in their vast sitting room. The light turned off and her mother screamed.

"You worthless woman, how dare you report me to the pastor?" Jane heard her father yelled, followed by a loud slap. She tried to focus her gaze on the image in front of her and moved closer to the ray of light at her front. Laying on the floor of the kitchen was her mother with hollowed eyes and blood dripping down from her head. Jane screamed and woke up from her nightmare. Her heart pounded loudly. Joe rushed into the room.

CHAPTER SIX

It was on a Thursday night, three days before Joe's leaving from home for the seminary, Joe and Jane had a big fight over their difference of opinions.

"It's a must you accept that job, Joe."

"I told you already, I can't take such a job. Besides, I am going to the seminary and will be there for sometime. I can't take up any job right now." Joe tried to reason with Jane.

"And you expect me to accept that as your silly excuse?" Jane stood at his front, glared at him with her arms akimbo.

"Please try to understand, love. I need to do this."

"To do what? Follow the non existing

believe?" Jane fired at him. "Fine, let me ask you this. If truly God speaks to you as you claimed and He wants the best for you, then why have I been barren for ten years now? Why haven't we had at least a child even though He knew how much we want a child of our own? Answer me?" She rained questions at him, screaming at the top of her voice.

"That's a test of faith, Jane," Joe defended.

"And which good father will test his children with such pain? It means He doesn't care about you, your pain or how you feel."

"Of course, He does, this is just for a little time."

Jane would have nothing of that, she continued. "A little you said, Mister, we have been married for ten years now, a decade with no child. Still, you kept saying everything will be fine. Your life is going from bad to worse, your career has probably hit the rock, your finance is zero. If not for I who bring in the money, we would have starved,"

"Then you should have bought a child

with your money," Joe blasted, losing his cool. He could not take the taunting anymore.

"Oh," Jane swallowed hard. It was as if Joe had just physically abused her with his response.

"So, you are blaming me now for our childlessness?" Her body shook with rage. Jane placed her left palm on her head to stop the sudden probing on her head. She tried to calm herself from going overboard.

"Then you are leaving for the seminary on Sunday?" Jane asked for the up tenth time.

"Yes," was his prompt reply.

"Alright then, I won't divorce you yet as you requested, but we have to separate for the time being."

"What is the difference between divorcing me and seeking separation from me?"

"Divorce signifies the end of our legal ties, granting us freedom from each other and relieving us of any obligations. For separation. I will still be your wife and you will still be my husband. Meaning none of us can marry someone else till we divorce each other legally, but we do not have to live together," the lawyer in her explained.

"I know all that already. What am asking is why are you separating from me? You said you are not giving me a divorce, but you don't want to be with me, either."

Jane shrugged her shoulder. "I am separating from you because I want you to have a deep thought about us and what you really want. If you want to be with me or your religion."

"I want you," cuts in Joe.

"No! You can't want me and still chose your religion over me. Make a choice between me and your faith."

"Your demand is unreasonable."

"I have made myself clear. I will give you all your three and a half years. You will stay at the seminary to think about this. Please respect my wish for no contact during our separation. You do as you please and I will live my life as I please. After the separation, if you are yet to decide or you decide to still hold on to your so-called faith or calling, you claimed to receive. Then I will have no choice but to divorce you. In 1st Corinthians 7:13, the Bible advises women not to divorce their non-believing husbands if they are happy to live together. And its verse 15 says, but if the unbeliever leaves, let it be so. The brother or the sister is not bound in such circumstances; God has called us to live in peace."

"But we are not unbelievers!"

"I am one," replied Jane.

"Just because I go to the church, don't make me a believer. I don't believe in all those religious jargon, so am considered an unbeliever. The Bible says you should let me go if I want to," Jane pointed out again.

"You are misquoting the Bible, Jane. I know you are a child of God, but you have been so hurt and your wound is deep. It makes you lose all sense of reason, but please don't take out your anger on me. Don't let me pay for the hurt of your father or every believer that has hurt you in the past," Joe pleaded with tears streaming down his eyes. He went on his knees. "Don't do this to me, please."

"Don't use that on me..." Her hands raised up. "I have made myself clear. We are separating for the time being," she sighed. "I just have a request from you." She looked at Joe, devoid of any emotion. "I want you to make love to me with a wild passion, even if this may be our last time together. Give me something to remember our relationship by, at the very least."

Joe looked at her face and saw the expression of a wounded lioness. He knew there was nothing he could say that would change her mind, and he questioned why he told God he wanted to marry such a cold-hearted soul.

Jane moved over to where Joe was sitting on the rug. She unbuttoned his shirt without waiting for his response, then moved to his trouser. She stood up to undress herself and right there she made love to Joe with a passion she has never displayed in all their ten years of marriage. Joe just laid down there on the rug. He was motionless, and he felt helpless and violated. Looking at Jane, he could see no form of emotion in her eyes. The act nauseated him. Joe wondered if Jane knew she was gradually turning into her father. She was also doing what her father did with her mother to him. The only difference in their cases was her father made use of both physical and verbal abuse of her mother, but Jane made use of verbal abuse more. And with this sex, it felt more like a violation of his body. Joe taught and tears streamed down his eyes, but Jane stared into space and continued with pleasing herself. When she had reached satisfaction, she picked up her cloth and undies on the rug, and went into the bedroom without a glance at Joe.

***

Jane woke up in the morning to find Joe gone. She had been feeling guilty ever since they made love in the sitting room. At least she didn't force him, she told herself. Jane tried to convince herself that nothing wrong had happened. As a wife, she had hundred percent right on her husband's body and she could do whatever she wanted with him, but why did the feeling of guilt persist? Jane felt she did something wrong. There was a nagging sound on her mind since then, but she felt too proud to talk to Joe and she didn't want him to think she was going soft because of his prayer.

Susan saw Joe in their sitting room, praying and sobbing throughout the night. She tried to justify her action, but all she could see was her mother's sad face, looking as if she was accusing her of being her father's daughter.

I'm not like him and I did nothing wrong. She muttered to herself. Jane closed her eyes and tried to block the intruding image.

***

Joe arrived at the seminary some minutes past two on Sunday afternoon. He dropped his luggage at Johnson, the security man's office.

It was with the help of Johnson; Joe got his admission into the seminary. They got to know each other on Joe's father's birthday because Johnson was a member of Joe's parents' church. Joe left Johnson's office and headed to the administrative office to see the registrar. Coincidentally, the registrar was Stephen Allen's acquaintance. They both did their pastoral training at The World Holy Trinity in Alaska.

"Hello sir."

"How are you doing, son?" Pastor

Adamson beamed his fatherly smile at Joe.

"I'm doing good, sir."

Pastor Adamson brought out a file from his second drawer and gave it to Joe.

"Go through it and sign on that page," he instructed and pointed to the last page.

"You can take a seat, son."

Joe sat down, flipping through the pages. He signed on the correct page and returned it to Pastor Adamson.

"What's the situation with Jane now?" Pastor Adamson gently asked.

"Still the same, sir, even if not worse," Joe replied with a sad face. Everything is crumbling and I'm unsure of how to mend it. I am helpless."

"God has everything under control, son. I don't want you to lose hope in your relationship. Keep praying and everything will be alright."

"But I've been doing that, sir. I've prayed and fasted, yet it's not working."

"Maybe you've been saying the wrong prayer," he pointed out to Joe.

"How?"

"You need to sit down calmly, reflect on

your relationship, on your life, on what attracted you to her. Reflect on your needs and your vision, then ask the Holy Spirit to give you the right prayer request. That's when you will start getting relief from your pain. But till then, read more of your Bible to understand more about the way of the Holy Spirit, how he communicates, and you will use it to turn your relationship back on the right track."

"Thanks sir," Joe appreciated him, stood up and left.

Joe went to the seminary chaplain to sign some papers, picked up his room key and went back to Johnson's office to get his bags

Joe made his way to the night chapel. He met the student chaplain and introduced Joe to other seminarians. Joe didn't know why, but he felt happy and alive to be among these people. It was the first-time people did not look down on him, rather; they wanted him to start a drama group at the seminary.

"Is that allowed in here?" It surprised him to hear such a suggestion from the student chaplain. To him, it was outrageous.

"Why not? Is there something wrong with acting at the seminary?" The student chaplain questioned Joe.

"I thought that's for the secular world and seminary is all spiritual," Joe retorted.

"We didn't ask you to go wild on us. Your acting should be based on good morals, principles, home building and on things that can make someone a better person. We need to spread awareness about the need for steadfastness and diligence in the things of the Lord. Besides, Jesus Christ made use of many parables that you can act on. It will make this place livelier," Andrew Hamsel, the student chaplain, told Joe. Others around supported Andrew and urged Joe to accept.

"What about the management? Will they accept it?" Joe felt reluctant to commit himself because he did not want to steps on the management toes.

"Leave that to me. I will take up the matter," Andrew assured him.

"Alright then, if you guys want," Joe agreed.

"Count me in, Joe," Cindy eagerly

volunteered to join the group. "Remember to include my name on the list," sounding excited.

"And me too," Sean, Cindy's husband puts in and they all bursted out laughing. Cindy and Sean Miles both came to the seminary together, and they were in their final year.

"It's fine by me if you all wish," Joe gave them a nod.

Joe was not expecting this show of interest in his career, especially in the seminary where he least expected it. He was glad the Lord led him here.

CHAPTER SEVEN

Joe joined the seminary over two years ago, but Jane still held on to the past. She kept comparing every man she came across with Joe. Jane realized that, when compared to other men, Joe was a saint despite his religious life that she found irritating and unbearable. She went out with Arnold Neil, a well-known broker she encountered at a club, seven months after Joe's departure for the seminary. Jane called Joe to tell him she had moved on and was interested in exploring a new relationship. Jane admits her error in getting involved with a devout man, fully understanding the challenge of separating him from his beliefs.

Jane inspected her pochette bag to

ensure it had all her essentials, closed the lid, and exited the room. As she was leaving, her mobile phone rang, and she retrieved it from her small bag.

"Hi Donald," Jane spoke into the handset.

"Have you left yet?"

"Yeah, I'll be with you soon."

"No, no," Donald quickly replied. "Something just came up," sounding desperate. Jane's posture stiffened.

"Don't tell me, you are backing out from this date again," Jane dared him.

"Settle down, Jane," sounding tipsy. "This is the problem I have with you. You easily get worked. Anyway, I got to go now, but I promised to make it up to you tonight," he assured. "I'll sleep over at your place tonight," Donald added, and blew her a kiss. He dropped the call without waiting for Jane's response.

The idea of a man sleeping over at Jane's house made her uneasy, especially given her experience.

***

It was on a weekend, Saturday night.

Jane felt so unhappy and didn't have anyone to turn to. At first, she wanted to call Mirabel, but she decided against it. Jane knew what Mirabel's response would be. Mirabel was against Jane's separation from Joe. Mirabel believed Joe was making the correct life choice and expected Jane to back him. To Jane, that advice was just like the one given to her mother when she went to report her father to Pastor James. It was the same advice that led to her mother's death. She didn't want to end up like her mum.

Jane picked up her phone, clicked on the browser, and searched for a nearby club. There were four clubs near her residence that she noticed, so she opted for the nearest one. Dressed in a denim sky blue jean, a black Bardot top and a black wedge to match her black saddle cross-body bag. She headed for the club, leaving her car at home. Jane boarded a cab.

Jane got to the club with the determination of forgetting herself in the excitement she may find herself and forget her sorrows.

"Hi beauty," a tall, dark man, probably

in his middle age, black hair, muscular body and of an average height walked up to her.

"Hello," Jane responded. Looking at him, she could see the distinct features of this man were so different from Joe's. She knew Joe could never have walked up to a random woman at the club, looking for friendship or a relationship either casual or permanent. Maybe she needed something different this time. Jane thought.

It was twenty-six minutes to eleven at night when Jane, slightly drunk, left the club with Alnold, and they both went to her house. She brought out her house key from her bag, inserted it into the door hole and they both went in. On getting inside, Jane collapsed on the sofa in her sitting room, out of exhaustion. Alnold took that as an invitation, without delay. He jumped on her. Though drunk, Jane knew perfectly well what she was doing and what her wants were. Jane was not the type of women a man could easily take an advantage of.

"No, not yet," Jane protested, dodging his unwelcome kisses.

"Come on babe, I know you want this,"

Alnold rebuffed her and plastered several kisses on her face.

Alnold and Jane heard the click on the doorknob, looking towards the door. Joe came in.

"It's not what you're thinking," Jane quickly said, trying to scramble out from the compromising position she was in.

"Hey, hey, hey babe wait, what the heck is this?" Alnold protested. He looked menacing at Joe. "And who the hell are you to barge in here just like that?"

"Quiet!" She looked rumpled, scrambling out from under Alnold and quickly standing up, brushing her disheveled hair away from her face.

Joe stood still, devoid of any emotion. He could not believe what he had just witnessed. Joe knew something terrible was going to happen that day. He could feel it in his spirit, but he did not know what it will be, and to witness this was more than he could take.

Joe looked at the man with Jane, then at Jane with her pitiful look. He gave a heavy sigh, picked up his bag that had fallen from his hand when he came in, opened the door and walked out, exchanging no word with Jane. He could hear Jane calling out his name.

"Listen to me Joe" Jane screamed after him, she made to run after Joe but Alnold blocked her way.

"Where do you think you are going?" Alnold demanded in a hoarse voice, trying to get closer to Jane. "You can't leave me hanging in the middle like this, baby."

Alnold grabbed Jane and tried to kiss her lips. Jane struggled out of his embrace and gave him a slap on his cheek.

"How dare you try to get close to me against my will? Didn't I tell you to stop that? Huh! See what you have caused now," she looked miserable. She brought her hand and rested it on her head, pacing the room. She looked very restless.

"And can you tell me who that was?" Alnold asked, visibly angry at the intrusion.

"That's my husband."

"What! You mean you are a married woman and still parades clubs looking for sex?"

"How dare you!" Jane blasted him. "Get

out of my house."

"Easy, girl. I'm just stating the facts here."

"Just get out I said!" She went to the door, opened it and gestured towards the door for Alnold to leave. Alnold got the clue, picked up his car key and angrily left.

"Damn you," he swore on his way out.

***

That was over a year. Jane had moved on with her life, though not entirely over Joe yet, but she has found another man for herself. Not just a man, she had gotten involved with several men after that escapade with Alnold, but all ended up wrong. The men she met either want her body on their first day of outing, which she refused to give in to their demands or her money. Two months ago, she met Donald. He seemed cool and caring, and he was the first man in these two years of her separation with Joe, who has not asked for sex. This was something significant to Jane. Donald was an attorney, but mostly dealt in criminal cases. He works in a big law firm at Ansell Law Firm, newly promoted as the head of the team and came to celebrate in the club with his friends when he met Jane. Still a bachelor and searching for the right woman according to what he told Jane. When Jane met Donald, he seems a serious type, and someone who loved his job.

He shared with Jane his aspirations of starting his own law firm and asked for her support. Jane agreed to help pay for his law firm bond, got him a building for his firm, and furnished the place. Shortly after that, Jane noticed the frequent absence of Donald. He had been ignoring Jane since he started his law firm, which he claimed took over two years owing to delayed fees.

I hope it's not what am thinking. Jane muttered to herself. She tried to calm herself down, feeling some sharp pain in her chest, "Ouch!" she screamed out of pain. Jane moved toward the kitchen. She took a glass cup and poured water on it. She drank it, but the pain grew sharp. Jane clutched her chest tight, slowly breath in and out, went down on her knees. She could still feel her heart slowly relieving from the pain, stood up and went to her bedroom to get some rest.

CHAPTER EIGHT

"**H**ow did you have the contract papers already?" Joe asked, feeling uneasy.

"I was at one of your rehearsals," Mr. Collins told him.

"Really, when? How?" Joe never expected someone to be so interested in him after he had nearly given up on himself.

"I invited him over to come and see you perform. He wanted to see your performance both on stage and off stage," Jones put in.

"And I like what I saw," Mr. Collins praised with a delightful approval.

This seemed so unreal to Joe. He had once wished for an opportunity like this where he could showcase his talent. Several times, he accepted a reduced fee for the sake of being in a movie, but none of his attempts were successful. Joe did not want his hope raised again and later have it come crashing down.

"Okay, sir, I will go through it and get back to you," Joe assured him. "Besides, everything is in God's hand," he added.

"We'll be happy to have you on board and if there're any changes you want, let us know. We'll definitely work something out," Mr. Collins told Joe.

Four days after Joe gave his career another chance, he called Mr. Collins' office and, after waiting on hold for some minutes, Hannah Luis, Mr. Collins' secretary, connected Joe to the boss. With the contract signing completed, Joe Allen arrived at the movie location two days before the production began.

The production crew was cooperative. Joe could not have wished for a better crew. Though it was not all rosy, they were some glitches during the lightning and five of the members had to isolate because of flu. Other than that, it was something to be grateful for.

"This calls for a celebration, boss," Annie

Rose cheered.

Everyone was ecstatic, but Joe sat in a corner, unable to digest his success. For three weeks in a roll, his movie has been in the number one spot in the box office and one of the most streamed Christian movie on several movie apps.

Joe reminisced about his life, from going to the seminary, separation from Jane, landing his first actual contract while still in the seminary and now, being a director and co-founder of a movie company, tears streamed down his eyes. If only Jane had understood him more and had little faith in him, they may still be together. Joe thought with a gloomy face.

Shortly after he graduated from the seminary, he ran into Jane at the cinema. She came with a friend. The movie showing was one of Joe's productions. From where Joe sat, he could see Jane's sorrowful face staring at the screen. He wished he could turn back their lives and how things went between them.

"Are you alright?" Annie asked Joe. She moved closer to wipe the tears from Joe's face.

Annie was Joe's secretary, as well as his confidant.

"I'm fine," Joe said, trying to move away from her.

"Joe, it's just the two of us. You can trust me and share anything," Annie whispered, inching closer.

Joe and Annie had become close friends. Annie longed for more, but he wasn't ready as his divorce from Jane was still pending.

"Will you like to go on a date with me tonight?" Annie asked, pleading with her eyes.

"You know I can't do that, Annie," Joe gently told her.

"But she has moved on," Annie persisted.

"We are still legally married. We have only separate, but not divorced yet," Joe pointed out.

"Then divorce her. After all, she doesn't give a damn about you," Annie urged.

"Jane is my wife and I love her," Joe muttered weakly.

"And you don't love me?" Annie asked.

"Can we end this subject, please?" Joe pleaded.

"Hell no, I need an answer," Annie insisted. "Don't you value my friendship and loyalty towards you all these years?"

Lost for words, Joe simply sighed.

***

Joe Allen never like to hurt anyone. He understood how it felt to be respected, but in this matter, he could not help it. Joe looked at Annie's tear-stained face. He felt sorry for her.

"Annie, calm down," Joe drew her in an embrace, trying to reason with her. I'm grateful for your support and care, especially when I'm feeling down. But it would be unfair to confuse our mutual understanding with love."

"But Joe..."

"Wait, Annie," he cut her off. "Yes, I love you."

"Really? You love me?" Annie's face lightened up, surprised to hear his confession.

"Yes, I love you, I really do, but, as a friend."

Annie gasped. She was not expecting such a response from Joe.

"As a friend?" She echoed. It felt like he

had just struck her by a moving train.

Joe knew that was not the reply she was waiting for, but he could not bring himself to lie to her. "I still love my wife and I hope we will get back someday."

"But she doesn't love you, and I do."

Annie tried to make Joe reason with her. She moved closer to Joe, embracing him and attempting to kiss him, but he turned his face away.

"Stop this Annie," Joe tried to free himself from her clutches, but she clung more to him.

"Stop it!" Joe shouted at her and jerked her hands off him. Her behavior left him displeased, obvious by his frown.

"I can't stay away from you anymore, even if you are married to that slut or not. You are mine, Joe." She clung to Joe and tried kissing him with a wild force.

Joe firmly grasped her and led her towards the door. "Stay here," he returned to collect her bag from the table and handed it to her.

"What are you doing?" Annie asked, her voice hoarse from sobbing.

"I think you are not in your right state of mind right now. We will talk when you are calmer, but always remember this. I will never leave my wife, and neither will I have an extra-marital affair." He narrowed his eyes at her and asked, "I hope you understand what am telling you?"

Annie smiled, shook her head, and turned back to Joe. "I think it will be better I get another job."

Joe was quiet. He didn't want her to depart in this manner, as he cherished their friendships.

"Is there no other way?" He desired to bring her joy, but he couldn't compromise his love for sympathy. It will later hurt them both.

Annie observed Joe's face and realized she had lost to Jane, a stranger whose name haunted her. Without responding to Joe's plea, she opened the door and left.

"Oh, my lord," Joe whispered and let out a long breath. He wondered why all his loved ones always choose to leave him.

***

Jane let herself into the house, switched

on the light, and went to the kitchen to make a light meal for herself. Her life had been a mess ever since Joe left, she thought miserably. Jane wished she had not reacted so mean to Joe. Now she would have still been married, Jane reminded herself.

She took out some eggs to make an omelet for herself, moving to switch on the gas cooker. Her heart squeezed as she felt her vision blur. She blacked out.

CHAPTER NINE

Jane, lying on the kitchen floor, could hear her mother calling her. She tried to reply, but her mouth felt too heavy to open. Jane wanted to sleep for a longtime but her mother's voice would not let her.

"Jane, open your eyes, please." Mirabel urged Jane.

"She will be fine, madam," the nurse assured Mirabel. 56-year-old Mary Barb understood Mirabel helplessness. "She will be up soonest."

"Thank you," came Mirabel's faint reply.

She had called Jane earlier, informing her she will spend the weekend with her. Mirabel's husband, Raymond, had gone on a business trip and their children had gone to spend the holiday at Raymond's parents' house. Mirabel was grateful to have such loving in-laws. They always treat her like their daughter and not like a daughter-in-law. She heard some stories about evil mother-in-law, but hers was the best. She could never have asked for a better one.

When she arrived at Jane's place, she knocked on the door, but Jane didn't respond. That looked strange to Mirabel. Since Mirabel could see Jane's car in the driveway, the question arose: where could Jane be?

Mirabel brought out her mobile phone and dialed Jane's number. It kept ringing without Jane answering. Mirabel could sense something was amiss. Jane's legs, tummy, and face were swelling, which concerned Mirabel, but she didn't want to frighten Jane without reason.

I hoped Jane is alright. Mirabel silently prayed.

She used the spare key Jane had given her a month ago to let herself into the house. She had asked Jane why she gave her the spare key, but Jane did not give her an actual answer. Jane simply said she just wanted her to have it.

"Thank God, I brought it along today," Mirabel whispered.

She entered the house and saw the lights were on. Is Jane home? She wondered.

Moving towards Jane's bedroom, Mirabel called out, "Jane!" Everywhere was silent. Walking up the stairs, she heard the ringing of a phone.

"That's from the kitchen," Mirabel muttered and headed to the kitchen. "Did she leave her phone at home?" Mirabel frowned, feeling uneasy. That was so unlike Jane.

Hearing the phone ring, Mirabel headed towards the sound and entered the kitchen to search for it. Her eyes wandered to the floor, where Jane remained motionless.

"Hello miss," a soft voice snapped her back to reality.

"Oh sorry, yes." She could see the doctor had been calling for her attention.

"I understand." He smiled at Mirabel with a sympathetic look on his face. On his breastplate was his name tagged; Dr. Hermes Clark.

"You are her relative right," he asked, wanting to be sure.

"Yes," Mirabel nodded, "I am like her sister. We grew up together at the house."

Dr. Clark understood where she was talking about. He did not dwell on that because he knew she was probably embarrassed to say it out.

"I understand she is married, right?" He asked again.

"Yes, but they are not together," Mirabel clarified.

She understood there was a serious issue by examining the doctor's face. She braced herself for the worse. "What is it?"

"Nothing is certain now," Dr. Clark began. "We need to conduct further tests, but from the echocardiogram test result, she has acute heart failure."

"What is that?" Jane mumbled; her voice is hoarse. She tried to sit up from her position, but looked exhausted. Mirabel and the doctor moved to Susan's side.

"Jane, you are awake." Mirabel touched Jane's hand with tears streaming down her face. She hugged Jane.

"What did the doctor say? Doctor?" Jane pressed the doctor for more information, keenly observing Mirabel's expression, realizing the gravity of the situation.

Mirabel could not hold back her tears. She wished she could make everything better for Jane. As a good friend, she had tried to persuade Jane to go back to Joe. She even tried to arrange reconciliation dates between both, but the guilt and shame of being caught with another man had held Jane back from accepting the dates. Mirabel knew Jane was merely keeping a brave face, but deep down, Jane felt lonely.

On the day Jane saw the announcement of Joe's movie nomination as the best movie of the year, she had come running to Mirabel in tears.

"It's my fault, Mirabel. I left a good man like Joe and went to those scumbags." Mirabel could still recollect Jane's agitated state and words. I underestimated his abilities. Despite my lack of support, he found success without me. Marabel, I betrayed his trust, hurt his feelings, and humiliated him. I acted like a monster. Mira,

I don't deserve his forgiveness."

Approaching Joe with a genuine heart will lead to his forgiveness. Don't give me that look, Jane. You admitted your mistakes, so why do you still feel the need to punish yourself?"

"That is what I deserve, Mira. He doesn't need someone like me by his side."

"That is for Joe to decide, Jane. Okay, let's meet with some church elders or Pastor Benson to intervene."

She pondered the outcome for Jane now. It's crucial for Jane to receive immediate treatment and have someone supporting her.

"What is it, Mira?" Jane asked again, bringing Mirabel out of the horrible thoughts going through her mind.

The doctor moved closer and lay a hand on Jane's shoulder. "There is nothing much to worry about," he studied Jane's reaction. "According to the report, you had a heart failure." Dr. Clark and Mirabel exchanged glances.

They observed Jane for any sign of shock but got none. Mirabel was confused, and she repeated. "The doctor said you had a heart failure. There's something wrong with your heart," Mirabel gently explained, thinking Jane must have been in shock not to reply.

"I know," Jane nodded slowly.

"What!" Mirabel exclaimed.

"I had it some month ago when I traveled to Texas. I had collapsed during a court hearing and rushed to the hospital." Jane was unmoved and her eyes cold.

"So... what happened?"

Jane averted her face from Mirabel's gaze. "The doctor said I had a heart attack, and I have been treating high blood pressure for sometimes now."

"Jane!" Mirabel shook her head. She would not believe what she just heard. "But you said nothing to me, and to think you considered me as your sister and best friend." Mirabel felt hurt hearing her friend had been suffering alone.

Jane looked from the young doctor to Mirabel. "That was the reason I visited you two months ago. Remember, I gave you my house key."

"So?" Mirabel shook her head, not getting what Jane was driving at.

"I could not bring myself to tell you. You have your worries, and you told me you are expecting another child."

"And what has that got to do with your health?" Mirabel queried.

"I know you will worry about me and with the state you are in, I don't want to put you under unnecessary stress." Jane looked lost.

Mirabel was helpless. She looked at the doctor with hope in her eyes. "Will there be a cure for this frequent health failure?"

"Miss or Mrs.?" He asked, wanting to know how to address her.

"Mrs." Not sure why that had to be important to put into consideration at this critical moment.

"Good," Dr. Clark muttered, "Mrs., we have to conduct some additional tests to understand why the frequent heart attacks, the causes and the best way to prevent or treat it." Mirabel and Jane exchanged glances. Jane nodded. She hoped for the best.

"Thanks doctor," Mirabel muttered to the doctor and Dr. Clark excused himself to attend to the other patients.

"Jane," Mirabel whispered and hugged Jane in a tight embrace. "I don't want to lose you," tears streamed down her eyes.

Jane could not keep up with the brave face. She burst into a deep sob, letting all her pent-up misery flow out. Her memories played out before her eyes, from childhood nightmares to her wedding day. Jane saw Joe's smiling face quickly turn to shock when he saw her with Alnold on that chaotic night.

"I'm I going to die?" Jane looked scared.

CHAPTER TEN

"**J**ust keep pushing, believe in yourself and have faith in God. Eventually, your hard work will yield results. Thank you all for having me." Joe concluded his speech.

Everyone applauded and stood up with loud cheers. Joe delivered a powerful speech. He had grabbed the attention of these five thousand young audiences at a conference organized by the Achievers World. After Joe's movie nomination, several doors opened for him and he had been attending one conference from the other. Within four months, he had traveled to fourteen countries for just forty-five minutes' talk in conferences and seminars.

Looking back at his life, Joe could not

believe it was the same him who many directors and actors had rejected in the past. Many of them had come back to his life. Some acted as if nothing ever happened, even claiming to be his best friends, while some had been remorseful enough to acknowledge their mistakes, but Joe was grateful to God. How he wished Jane had been here to share in his happiness and success. He still misses Jane, so much it hurts. Joe thought, feeling a bit dejected.

A year ago, Mirabel had contacted him in order to reconcile him with Jane. He wished for that also, but he had objected to the movie. Yes, he still loves Jane, Joe told Mirabel, but that did not mean he had forgotten what Jane did to him. Jane betrayed his trust and made a mockery of their marriage, yet she never apologized for her wrongdoing.

To Joe, getting back with Jane would have been a disregard for him and he must maintain his self-respect. Coming together with him and Jane this time around must be something both Jane and he wanted.

Joe blamed his one-sided love for the

pain and heartbreaks he experienced. If Jane had at least loved him halfway, she would not have been so cold towards him. He had accepted Jane's faithless state because he loved her, but for her to ridicule his faith was uncalled for.

"That was such a powerful speech, Mr. Joe." Mr. Emmanuel Hounda brought his hand forward for a shake.

"Thank you so much," Joe replied, equally accepting Mr. Emmanuel Hounda's shake. Both had met at another conference in France. Mr. Emmanuel Hounda was the speaker on the second day and instantly hit it off with Joe when they met at the dinner table.

"I want to introduce you to some important guests. They are dying to meet you," Mr. Hounda told Joe.

Joe followed him to meet his important guests.

"Dad!" Joe exclaimed. He could not believe his eyes. "Dad, are you here?" He looked totally surprised to see his father at the conference.

"Of course, son, I am here in flesh and

blood," Stephen Allen replied his son. He stood up and embraced Joe. "I miss you, son."

"And won't I get to see my son also?" A female soprano voice said from behind. It shocked Joe to hear the voice.

"Mum!" Joe couldn't hold his emotion at seeing his mother. His eyes widened, and he stayed rooted to the same spot.

"Come on here," Linda Allen gestured to Joe with her open arms. Joe rushed on for a tight embrace. She gave Joe a kiss on both cheeks. "I miss you, son."

"I miss you too, mom, dad," Joe responded with unconcealed emotion.

Joe turned to Mr. Hounda. "Have you met my parents before?"

"Of course, son," he answered. "Hearing your last name and seeing you reminded me of my good friend Stephen," Mr. Hounda responded. Joe looked at his dad. Mr. Hounda's statement confused him.

"We crossed paths in jail during my embezzlement accusation. You were still a kid then," his father chipped in.

"I remember that time." Joe turned to Mr. Hounda. So, this man too was once a convict? He thought silently.

As if reading Joe's mind, Mr. Hounda smiled. "The judge convicted me of attempted rape and gave me seven years' jail term." Mr. Hounda saw the shocked expression on Joe's face. He laughed out loud.

"Do you think I have always been a saint?" He teased. "Well, the same lady the court sent me to prison for was the same person who converted me. She came to the prison to preach to me to change my ways. She is my wife now," he added.

"What!" Joe shouted. "Are you for real?"

Mr. Hounda winked. "I was in love with her so I could do anything for her, anyway after my time in jail, we got married. We have six children to make up for all my lost time," he ended.

"He was the one that lead me to Christ," Joe's father put in.

"I see." Joe simply nodded his head. The story moved him.

Joe's phone rang. He checked the screen for the caller's name, but there was none.

"Hello," Joe said after picking up the call.

"Mirabel speaking," Mirabel responded

tensely.

She looked at the unconscious Jane lying down on the hospital bed with a ventilator connected to her nose and a drip attached to her body. Mirabel took a deep breath, with tears in her eyes and her voice quaking.

"Jane is dying." Mirabel blurted out.

Joe Allen felt the ground pulled out from his feet and everywhere went dark.

"What did you say?" Joe muttered faintly.

"What is it, Joe?" his mother asked. Joe's devastating look made it seem like he had just been sentenced to death."

"Joe, come here as fast as you can. The doctor said Jane's life is at risk unless we find a heart donor in time." Mirabel could not hold back her despair.

Joe went quiet, leaving Mirabel unsure if he was still there. She found herself in a state of complete confusion once more. How could she lose her friend like that? She asked in despair and to no one in particular.

"Are you still there?" She wanted to be sure if Joe heard her.

Joe took a deep breath. "I don't understand what you are saying, but just hold on there. I will take the next flight and meet you there. Send me your location," he added, and cut the line.

"What is it, son?" his father moved closer and placed his hand on Joe's shoulder.

Joe did not answer. In fact, he could not fully understand what Mirabel just said, and he tried to absorb it.

"I have to go back now. Jane is in the hospital. She needs me," he told them.

"But what is the problem?" his mother tried to get more information from him.

"It's alright, son. You can go," his father gave his mother a look to stop her from protesting. Looking at Joe's state, Stephen knew he needed to be alone and Mr. Hounda understood that.

"God be with you, son," Mr. Emmanuel Hounda prayed.

Joe got on the next available flight. He prayed like he had never prayed in his entire life, yet he kept getting horrible flashes of Jane dying.

Please Lord, he prayed with his whole heart.

The one and half hour flight from New York back to Boston with all airports protocol seemed like an eternity to him. He was losing his mind and unable to stay calm. Joe picked up his mobile phone, he dialed Raymond's number.

"Yes Joe," Raymond answered his call on the other line.

"How is she?" Joe asked his friend.

"She is still unconscious. The doctor said they hope she comes around soon else," Raymond stopped, he could not utter the word.

"Else what?" Joe probed, knowing the answer already.

"Just get here fast," Raymond urged.

"Soon," Joe answered.

Joe arrived at the hospital and met Raymond with Mirabel at the reception, holding onto each other. They stood up when they saw him. Mirabel's face was red and swelled up from crying.

"Raymond, Mira, thanks for being here for Jane." Joe gave Mirabel a hug. "It is okay Mira, everything will be alright, and you need to pull yourself together for Jane," Joe told her.

"I've been trying to tell her that, especially in her state," Raymond puts in. Joe looked at Mirabel again.

"Is she sick?" Joe asked Raymond.

"No, no," Raymond responded. "She's pregnant," he clarified.

"Oh! Congratulations," pleased with the news. "I'm happy for you guys." Joe hugged Raymond, but Mirabel simply burst into a fresh sob.

"Calm down, darling," Raymond pleaded. He looked miserable.

"Where's the doctor?" Joe asked Raymond after Mirabel's sob subsided.

"We'll take you to him," Raymond offered. They went to see the doctor in charge of Jane's treatment for a better explanation.

Raymond stayed by Jane's bedside in the ICU, holding Jane's hand. Raymond had taken Mirabel home when she had gone hysterical after the doctor told them Jane needed a heat transplant urgently, else she would die in a couple of weeks. According to the doctor, Jane had a hole in the heart after she had a heart failure. Three heart failures within five months had weakened her heart and affected her lungs and organs badly. She must stay on life support till she could undergo a heart surgery. This brought them to a greater problem. Where would he find a heart for her?

CHAPTER ELEVEN

Joe reminisced back to all the good times he shared with Jane. Will it all end just like this? Joe mournfully asked. Just then, he saw Jane's hand shook.

"Jane?" He whispered her name.

Jane opened her eyes and looked around. Confused about her surroundings, then it came flooding back to her. Jane remembered she had been talking to Mirabel when her breathing became difficult and she started gasping for breath. Jane tried to remember what happened after that when she noticed someone in the room. Moving her head to the left side, she could not believe who was there.

"Joe!" she muttered. The ventilator prevented her voice from being audible. Joe quickly pressed the alarm button by Jane's bedside to alert the medics about Jane's state, and within some seconds, they rushed in.

"I need you to go out please," a doctor said to Joe. About five of the hospital staffs gathered around Jane; a male doctor and three female nurses, with one male nurse. Joe slipped out of the ICU with a heavy heart.

Joe sat outside of the ICU with his chin rested on his palms. He felt lost. Joe wondered if he was going to lose Jane, but he believed in a miracle. Yes, only a miracle could save his love.

"Help me Lord."

"Mr. Allen," Dr. Clark gently called Joe. He was oblivious to his surrounding. "You can go in now to see her, but make sure she doesn't get too excited," Dr. Clark advised.

Joe thanked the doctor and went to see Jane. On sighting Joe, Jane attempted to stand up from her sleeping position, but Joe quickly moved to her side. He steadied her and made her sit up a bit.

"Are you comfortable?" Joe asked her,

feeling cosigned.

Jane could not bear the sympathetic look on Joe's face. Unstoppable tears rolled down her face.

"Don't cry, Jane." He understood her tears.

"I am sorry Joe, so so sorry," Jane blurted out between her sob.

"It's alright Jane, remember you are in a delicate state," Joe pacified her, giving her a gentle pat on her shoulder.

"I betrayed you, yet you came to see me," Jane castigated herself more. "I am sorry, Joe," she kept pleading.

"Calm down Jane, I have forgiven you a long time," Joe told her. He placed her free hand on his palm and gently caressed it.

"To err is human, Jane, and as a believer, to forgive is divine. I have forgiven you, darling."

"But I messed up."

Joe reached out and stroked her hair. "I know, but not you alone. We both messed up and am sorry too. I could not give you the life you deserve."

"I should have believed more in you," she

retorted. "And now it's too late. I'm dying." Jane wept silently.

"No Jane," Joe tried to give her some hope, "If you believe in the Lord, he can save you," he told her.

"Lord?" Jane asked. "But I don't know him. I don't even know if he truly exists," she moaned.

"He exists, Jane. He changed my life. The Lord can also save your life if you give him a chance."

"I'm messed up right now, Joe."

"Not as messed up as Mary Magdalene, the Lord is always ready to wash the dirty off the dirtiest." He dabbed her face with his handkerchief.

"What do I have to do?" Jane lifted her face with a small ray of hope in her eyes.

Joe smiled at her. "Close your eyes and say after me."

Jane closed her eyes and folded her hands together. She repeated his words of confession, "Lord Jesus, I know that am a sinner and I am sorry for my sins. Forgive me and accept me as your own. Amen." She opened her eyes and smiled shyly at Joe, who reached out to her and kissed her lightly on the lips.

"I feel tired," Jane yawned.

Joe went out of the room for Jane to have a quiet sleep.

"Dad, mum," Joe sighted his parents as they came into the room. He stood up to give each a hug.

"How are you, son?" Stephen Allen looked tired.

"I am holding up dad," Joe replied with a sad smile. Linda and Stephen Allen flew in from New York to see Jane and support their son. They knew how Joe loved Jane and this was a trying period for Joe.

"How is she?" Linda gestured towards Jane. She looked so helpless, lying on the hospital bed.

"She's been sleeping since yesterday. I'm kind of getting worried," Joe sighed.

"Have you called the doctor to come check her?" Stephen asked.

"I did, dad. The doctor said she's alright, just sleeping but who sleeps for sixteen hours straight except in a comma," by now he's almost shouting at the top of his voice.

"Lower your voice, son. Everything will be alright." Stephen drew Joe into a tight embrace, giving him a pat on the back.

Linda bent down and gave Jane a peck on the cheek. "Get well soon, love."

***

Jane opened her eyes to see she was in a dark tunnel. Up ahead was a ray of light, so she followed the light. Jane saw a ladder at the edge of the tunnel leading up, probably to an open ground. She climbed it and coming out of it was a narrow path. Jane came out of the cave like tunnel and followed the path. Dressed in a with flowery gown, she had no sandals on her feet.

Coming out of the narrow path, Jane saw some sheep by a riverside, drinking water from the river brooks, and she ran to it. Jane scooped some water up with her palm and drank it and splashing some on her face.

"Oh!" Jane exclaimed. "What a relief," she muttered cheerfully.

Jane looked around the place. It looked so beautiful and serene.

"Where is this place?" she wondered. Jane had never felt at peace like this in her life.

"But how did I get here? Wasn't I in the hospital with Joe?" Jane asked to no one in particular.

"Joe! Joe!!" Jane called out, running around searching for Joe.

Jane stood still, looking lost and confused. "Where am I?"

Jane saw some sheep moving away from the river and in another direction. She followed them.

***

"Wake up Jane," Joe pleading with the sleeping Jane. His parents had waited for a long time hoping to talk to Jane when she wakes up but left after the doctor had told them she had fallen into a deep sleep. According to Dr. Clark, Jane did not wish to wake up.

"Failure to find a heart within 72 hours," Dr. Clark shock his head. "We might lose her as her organs are failing." After Dr. Clark left the room, Joe went on his knees and buried his head in Jane's stomach. He shed bitter tears.

***

Jane followed the sheep, hoping to meet someone along the way. To Jane, it seemed strange with the sheep's movement. They all head in the same direction with no shepherd leading them and they all seemed to have a mutual understanding with where they were going. Suddenly, the sheep turned left and went on a cliff. Jane hesitated. Should she follow or not? She thought. Looking around again with no one in sight, she followed the sheep.

***

Joe woke up startled and witnessed the room in a state of commotion. Several medical personnel gathered around Jane, trying to resuscitate her. Joe did not know what to think of the drama happening at his front, and the sound of the breathing machine was driving him crazy. To stop the assault on his mental state, he put his hands on his head, open his mouth and let out a deafening wail.

CHAPTER TWELVE

Joe yelled at the top of his voice. He could not withstand the pressure of his mental state anymore.

"Someone should take him out fast," a doctor ordered. Two orderly lead Joe out of the room and made him sit in the reception, reassuring him everything will be alright. Joe felt helpless. He wanted to do more, but he did not know how to make thing better for Jane.

"Hello Joe Allen, how is your wife doing now?" Joe heard a lady asked. He looked up into the unfamiliar face and saw some reporters flashing their cameras at him with about dozens of microphones pointing to his mouth. Joe was at a loss for words.

"There's a report circulating that your wife is in serious condition. Your fans will like to know the situation and how they can help?" The reporter asked.

"Oh... well," trying to comport himself, "Jane is in the ICU. She needs a heart transplant, and the doctors said if she doesn't undergo surgery on time, we might lose her," Joe said with a teary face. "I need all your prayers for my wife. I love her and don't want to lose her."

"Thank you for your time and we hope you get all the help needed," another reporter said.

"Thank you," Joe gave a slight bow with his hand on his chest.

Joe turned back to check on Jane again when he saw Mirabel coming into the hospital with Raymond. He waved his left hand at them.

"How is Jane?" Mirabel looked frightened. The reporters she saw obviously disturbed her. "Is Jane alright?" she asked with bathed breath.

"The doctors were trying to resuscitate her, the last time I was in the room."

"What!" Mirabel exclaimed; her eyes widened with fear. She dashed towards the ICU, not minding her condition.

"Mira, wait," Raymond called after her.

Mirabel raced to where Jane was, fearing for the worse, and Raymond swiftly moved to catch up with her.

"You should not be running in this state," Raymond scolded.

"Please," Mirabel pleaded, not in the mood for lectures, especially with her friend dying.

They waited outside the ICU, observing what's going on through the glass partition. After sometime, the doctors eventually got Jane's heart under control and Dr. Clark came out to meet the distraught Joe.

"You look so handsome today, Mr. Joe," Dr. Clark teased. Joe managed a sad smile.

"I wish I am," Joe replied. "How is she?" gestured towards Jane.

"She's stable now," Dr. Clark informed Joe. He looked at Mirabel. "You should take things easy, madam. Everything will be fine," he told Mirabel.

"Take care of her," Dr. Clark told

Raymond.

"You can all go inside to see Jane. Let me know if you observe any changes in her movement," he instructed.

"Alright doctor, thanks for your help," uttered Joe.

"You are welcome," Dr. Clark replied and left.

"I want to go get some fresh air," Joe told Mirabel and Raymond. "You guys can go ahead."

"I will come with you," Raymond promptly said. He could not risk leaving Joe alone in his state.

"I am actually fine."

"I know. I just want to come with you," Raymond insisted.

"Alright then," Joe succumbed.

"Go along darling, we will be back soon," Raymond told Mirabel. She understood Joe's mood and felt sorry for him.

Joe and Raymond strolled aimlessly for thirty minutes, exchanging no word. Raymond allowed Joe to explore his misery uninterrupted, a thing he must do in order to overcome his grief. With his hands on his knees, Joe burst into a sudden, deep sob. Raymond gently placed his hands on Joe's shoulder in support.

"Let it all out. Scream if you feel like, just let it all out and you will be back to normal," Raymond assured his friend.

"I love her despite everything," Joe wailed.

"I know, and am sorry for everything you are going through, Joe."

"But why didn't she tell me she's suffering? I would have come running to her. Now everything is too late."

"Nothing is late, brother. If you have faith even as small as a mustard seed, Jane will be alright."

"But why didn't she call me back?" Joe punched his palm.

"Because she hated her father, and she believed she had turned out like him."

"So?" Joe could not see the relation between hating her father and coming back to him.

"Jane told us how she violated you."

Joe went pale, and he tried to find the right words to say. He felt embarrassed to admit his wife's violation of his body.

"It's alright Joe. I know how you feel." Raymond moved closer to Joe and placed his hand on his shoulder. Raymond led Joe to a nearby chair at the community playing ground.

"I just want you to know how much Jane regretted that. After you left for the seminary, she couldn't live with the guilt. Mirabel tried to make her come to you. In Jane's word, you deserve someone better."

"I would have forgiven her immediately if she had only asked," Joe wept, placing his face on his palms.

"I know, but Jane wanted to punish herself for her dad's action. Jane thought she had become a monster like her dad and she couldn't leave with that." Raymond wrapped his hands around Joe's shoulder. "I'm glad you came back."

Joe could not hold his emotion anymore. He embraced Raymond and wept.

***

Jane followed the sheep to the cliff top. She saw an elderly man with a gray beard dressed in a white robe, and he was holding a walking stick.

Jane stood still, watching the old man from afar, and wondering how the old man got to be here alone with these sheep. The old man seemed to be aware of Jane's presence. Without turning to Jane, he called out to Jane.

"Hi Jane!"

It startled Jane. "How do you know my name?" Jane asked, moving a little closer to the old man and trying to see his face.

He turned to Jane and smiled. "I have been waiting for you, daughter."

"Daughter?" She repeated, confused. "Are you my grandpa?" The old man chuckled.

"What are you doing here? And I remembered my mother said you died when I was a baby. Did she lie to me? And why don't I remember how I got here?" Jane bombarded him with questions.

"Where do you think you are?" He responded with another question.

Jane studied her surroundings. "This place doesn't look like anywhere I know or have seen before. Or... am I dead?" She whispered with her eyes widened.

The old man laughed out loud. "Do I look like a dead man to you?"

"An old man with many sheep. You look too neat for a shepherd," she responded.

"Why is that?" he queried Jane, looking curiously at her.

"Well, your cloth is too neat for a shepherd," she gestured to the old man's white garment.

"Good observation," he answered gently. "Inspect the sheep," he ordered Jane.

Jane turned towards the sheep. She inspected them thoroughly, but she could find nothing strange or out of line. She looked back at the old man.

"I saw nothing out of the ordinary," she replied, glancing back at them. "Except they look clean than the usual sheep I see about," she added.

"Exactly, daughter," the old man nodded, smiling at Jane. She noticed his white teeth.

Is he actually my grandpa? Jane wondered.

"I am neat because my sheep are clean," he told her.

"Oh!" Jane whispered. "You are right."

The sheep moved to the old man's back and came together.

"Can I ask you a question?"

He nodded. "Go on."

"I have not seen you talk to them, but they seem to know what you want without telling them, where to go and how do you get them so clean? It must have been difficult with these lots." It amazed Jane, seeing the movement of the sheep.

The old man beckon to Jane to move closer, he whispered to her eyes.

"Because they know me."

Jane drew back. For some reasons Jane could not figure out, she found this old man strange. Looking nervously at him, her heart started pounding so hard.

"How is your father?"

"I don't know," Jane tensed.

"Why is that, or you don't care?" His eyes probing.

Jane folded her palm tensely. "I have nothing to do with him," she replied.

"Walk with me," the old man ordered.

Jane and the old man walked for some

minutes silently before the old man turned to her. "Why are you hurting yourself for your father's mistake?"

Jane felt sure this was not her grandfather.

"You are not really my grandpa," she pointed out. "Did my father told you about me?"

"That is not important, Jane. You need to let go of the past."

"No! Never, I can't do that," Jane shook her head. "He hurt my mother and killed her." Jane retorted with tears threatening to fall out.

"What about Joe? Why are you punishing him?" He queried her.

It's not my intention to punish him. Joe means everything to me, but I don't think I'm deserving of his love."

"You should let him decide that, not your decision to make."

"I don't want him to go through what my mother passed through." Jane defended her actions.

Your mother is content in her current state and wishes for your happiness, too.

"How do you know that?"

The old man held Jane by left arm, and he gestured towards a doorway. "Come, let's go to see your mother."

CHAPTER THIRTEEN

Jane saw her mother holding a watering can in the middle of a garden, looking so radiant.

"Mom!" Jane called out.

"She can't hear you."

"What do you mean she can't hear me?" Jane turned to the old man. "Mummy!" Jane called to her again.

Jane jerked her hand away from the old man's hand and ran to her mother, only to collide with an invincible wall. She tumbled to the floor.

"Mummy!"

The old man moved closer to Jane and bent down to her eyes level. "Why are you putting yourself under undue pain, Jane?"

Jane got scared and cringed back from him.

He moved towards her. "You've piled up so much bitterness in your heart that you lost your peace." He bent down again, closer to her ear. "The pain of your mother's memory consumed you so much that you forgot love and embraced hatred."

Jane stood up and tried to bolt, but she realized she could not move. Jane looked down at her feet and tried to move it, but her feet were stuck to the ground.

The old man moved closer, and he continued. "Your hatred for all men spread all over your vein, and your blood boiled over for anything that has to do with love. It affected your heart. It knocked it out."

He brought his mouth closer to Jane's face and whispered. "Now you have just some minutes left. The doctors will pull off the ventilator and..." he snapped his fingers. "You will be no more, all because of your bitterness," he moved back from her.

"What do you want from me?" Jane muttered, panting.

"Nothing, nothing Jane," he replied.

He steadied his gaze at Jane. "The doctors are about to switch off the ventilator."

"What? Doctors, what doctors?" Jane panicked. She could not understand what he was referring to.

"Where are you?"

"Here with you, of course," Jane replied.

"No, no, no," he shook his head. "Think again with a calm mind. Close your eyes, concentrate on your surrounding and search deeply."

Jane went still and closed her eyes. She saw Joe on his knees, praying and weeping. Jane tried to survey the room, but it was dark. She looked closely, and she saw herself on the bed with a breathing machine attached to her nose.

***

Dr. Clark came into the room and saw Joe on his knees. He gently tapped Joe on his shoulder.

"Sorry to interrupt, but I need to discuss this with you," he told Joe.

Joe got up from his knees, his eyes puffy from lack of sleep, coupled with too much weeping.

"What is it, doctor?"

"We have deliberated on Jane's case and most agreed we switch off the life support attached to her," Dr. Clark informed Joe.

"No! You can't do that," Joe countered. "She is not dead yet."

"There's no use leaving her like this. She is not responding to treatment," Dr. Clark gently pointed out.

"I believe my lord will bring her back. Jesus promised me she will not die but live. Jane is not dead," Joe insisted.

"I am sorry Mr. Joe, if she doesn't wake up in the next 24 hours, we will switch off the machine," Dr. Clark replied.

"You can't do that," Joe protested, holding on to the doctor's hand.

"I need to attend to other patients please," Dr. Clark excused himself.

Joe collapsed on the floor. "Lord, I need you now. Help me please," Joe pleaded.

***

"Help me please, I need to go back," Jane pleaded with the old man. "I can't die just like this. Joe needs me," she added.

"Joe needs a woman he can love and will

love him, too. Not someone full of bitterness," the old man pointed out. Jane went on her knees, pleading and weeping.

"Forgive me, please," she pleaded.

"That is not the right word, Jane," he told her. "It is not about me forgiving you, but you forgiving your dad," he told her.

"My dad again?" She asked. "And who are you?"

"I'm the one who you hate so much. Because of your dad, you do not wish to have anything to do with me. You come to sing in the church, but you hate me who owns the church."

"You own the church? Are you him? Jesus," she muttered faintly. "I thought you were never real," her face registered shock. Jane grabbed his legs, crying on his feet.

"I am sorry lord, forgive me. I was ignorant," she pleaded. "Yes, I hated my father because he caused my mother so much pain and many people who I thought were good also hurt me and I thought if you were real, you would have saved me. My mother believed in you, yet she died like that. But now my mom is happy and am sad. I am sorry, so sorry," she wept.

The old man placed his hand on Jane's head. "It's alright, child. Go back and make everything alright," he told her.

Jane looked at him with hope in her eyes. "Really, but isn't it rather too late? I am dying."

"Don't you remember my word? Seek first my kingdom and righteousness with it, then you will receive every other thing you may need."

"Your kingdom and righteousness? How?"

"Forgive and love."

***

"Doctor!" Joe exclaimed. He pointed to Jane on the bed. "S... she just moved her fingers."

The doctor swiftly moved into action to check Jane. She kept shaken her finger and tried to open her eyelids. Joe stood still, observing the doctor and hoping for some good news. Jane opened her eyes.

"Look at her, doctor," Joe jumped in excitement.

Jane muttered something, but her words were inaudible.

"She's saying something," Joe told the doctor.

"What is it?" Dr. Clark asked. Jane kept moving her lips, but they could not understand what she was saying. Joe bent down and brought his ear closer to her mouth.

"What is it, Jane?" Joe asked again.

Jane turned her head towards Joe, and she whispered to him. "Old man, I saw the old man."

Joe looked confused. He brought his ear closer to Jane's month; he focused on her words.

"I saw the old man," Jane muttered again.

Joe turned to the doctor. "She is talking about an old man. I don't know what that means."

"She must be in delirium," Dr. Clark replied. Just then, the life-support machine attached to Jane started beeping faster and Jane was grasping for breath. Dr. Clark pressed the alarm bell bedside Jane's bed. Within some seconds, several medical personnel rushed into the room.

"We are losing her," one doctor said.

Joe stood rooted to the spot.

Some minutes ago, he was happy she finally gained consciousness, but in a jiffy, she seemed to slip away from his grip right before his eyes and he could do nothing.

A doctor came into the room and went to Dr. Clark. "A fax came in now," he informed Dr. Clark. "We have found a heart and they are on the way here."

"Good," Dr. Clark responded. "But we need to stabilize her first," he added.

They tried to regulate Jane's heart beat.

"When will the heart arrive?" Asked another doctor.

"Approximately in 15 minutes' time," replied the elderly doctor.

"We should get her into the operating room then," another doctor said.

"Yes," Dr. Clark replied. "I hope she makes it till then," he added.

Turning to Joe, "Wait outside please," Dr. Clark instructed Joe.

Joe moved outside. He brought out his mobile phone from his trouser front pocket and dialed his father's number.

"Dad, where are you?" Joe asked tearfully.

"We are on our way, son," Stephen Allen replied his son. "Is Jane alright?" He asked, sounding consigned.

"I don't know, dad; I don't want to lose her and I don't want her to die," Joe cried, dropping his phone on the floor.

"Hello? Son? Joe?" His father called out, but he did not receive any response.

"Help me, Lord, bring Jane back," Joe pleaded, with tears running down his face.

"Joe," he heard Mirabel's voice called out his name. Mirabel and Raymond arrived to see some fans outside the hospital weeping and holding placards on their hands with condolences messages on it.

"What was that I saw outside?" Mirabel pointed outside with a shaken finger and tears threatening to gush out of her eyes. "Don't tell me she's... Jane... she's dead?" Mirabel muttered. She looked so frightened and vulnerable.

"I don't know... I mean, not yet. They rushed her into there," pointing to the operating room.

"Thank God," Raymond whispered in relief.

"But those placards?" Mirabel gestured towards the door.

"Forget them," Raymond told her. He drew her closer and tried to get her to sit down.

"Everything will be alright," Raymond assured Mirabel.

"I hope so," Joe responded.

Joe saw his parents walked in frantically, probably searching for the operating room. The receptionist must have told them Jane was in the operating theater. Joe thought.

"Son," Stephen called, embracing his son.

"Dad, Mon." Joe went into their open arms. He sensed his mum has been crying. Her eyes looked red and puffy, but she maintained a straight face.

"She will be fine, Joe," Linda assured his son. Joe knew she probably said that in order to console herself.

CHAPTER FOURTEEN

Dr. Clark and two other doctors rushed out of the operating room as they heard the door open. Dr. Clark remained with Joe after the other two doctors hurried off.

"Mr. Joe," Dr. Clark said. "There seems to be a change in the situation."

They all went pale, but Stephen Allen braced himself for the worse, and he asked. "What is the issue, doctor?"

"We don't seem to understand what is going on."

"Like what, doctor?" Joe's heart pounded in a rapid race.

"Is she dead?" Mirabel uttered under her breath.

"Of course not," Dr. Clark responded. "It's something else."

He felt sorry for them, looking at all their faces. "We need to conduct some new tests on her."

"Okay, but why?" With one hand gripping tightly, Joe wiped the sweat off his face. "What about the heart donated? Didn't it match Jane's?"

"That's not the problem," the doctor responded.

"The what is it, doctor?" Mirabel held on tight to her husband's hand.

"There was never actually anything wrong with Jane's heart, it seems," he said.

They all exchanged confused glances.

"What do you mean, doctor?" Joe pondered how that came to be.

Dr. Clark's gaze filled with unease as he looked at them. We need to perform additional tests on her to be sure. Can you join me to sign some papers?

Joe sank to his knees, hands lifted in joy. "Hallelujah! Dad, mom, Raymond, this is a miracle." In one swift motion, he jumped up, hugged his father, then his mother, and finally let out a loud scream, oblivious to his surroundings.

Dr. Clark struggled to keep his expression neutral. "We need to be certain, please," he insisted.

"Let's go," Joe stood up. Feeling ecstatic, he took the doctor's hand and led him away.

At 5:25pm, Dr. Clark, along with two other doctors, came to meet Joe and discuss their findings. The test's outcome had Mirabel, Raymond, and Joe's parents on edge. As they approached, Joe stood up from his seat and the others did the same.

"Mr. Joe," began Dr. Mark, the elderly doctor. "We completed all the required tests, but pinpointing the exact changes remained elusive. We were certain she had a serious heart condition which needed urgent surgery. But now, the situation has changed."

Dr. Clark cleared his throat. "Just as I told you earlier, there doesn't seem to be any health issue with her. Jane's heart, organs, blood pressure are in perfect condition."

"What does that mean?" Stephen asked with bated breath.

"She doesn't need a surgery anymore,"

responded the third doctor.

"She is perfectly fine," Dr. Clark put in.

"Ah!" Joe leaped up, clapped his hands, and then threw a punch in the air. They could not believe their ears and we're all overjoyed.

"Though we still have to observe her for some days or weeks, at least to understand what happened," Dr. Clark told them.

"It was a miracle that happened, doctor," Joe retorted. "It was a miracle," with tears streaming down his face. Linda held onto her husband, crying silently. Raymond hugged Mirabel and gently patted her on the back, soothing her tears. They could not withhold their emotions. Dr. Mark gave them permission to go in and see her.

Jane stayed for two more weeks at the hospital while the doctors conducted more tests on her. Most of the doctors did not want to admit the change in Jane's conditions to any religious belief of Joe, yet they admitted to the strangeness of the case. None could explain what happened or how it happened, but Jane and Joe felt sure it was the Lord who healed her. Jane narrates her encounter with the old man to Joe and vowed to make peace with her father the moment she leaves the hospital. Joe sat on the bed with Jane, and holding her close.

"What is the secret you were hiding all these years?" He asked.

"Can't we just forget that?" She had a pleading look on her angelic face.

Joe smiled, placed a kiss on her lips to ease her fear. "Don't hold back, my love. Let it all out. I don't want anymore secret between us. Open up the pain, let go of bitterness, and allow forgiveness to heal you. Only then will you experience true freedom.

She sighed, closed her eyes and went back to that memory lane. To her childhood worst nightmare.

Jane remembered coming home with her parents that day from the Friday bible study. Her mom had earlier reported her father to Pastor James, but he had shut her mother up. On getting home, her dad unleashed his anger on her mother and she could remember her mother ran into the kitchen.

"How dare you report me to the pastor,"

Desmond charged towards Susan, giving her a hard kick.

"Do you think the pastor will report me to the police?" He let out a sarcastic laugh.

Jane recalled her father boasting about his wealth and importance in the church. She approached the kitchen door, her legs trembling, and witnessed her mother writhing in agony on the floor, blood flowing from her head.

Desmond, her father, looked at her with a sly smile. He unbuttoned his shirt, then pulled down his trouser. He stooped down next to her mom and flipped up her gown. Right on the kitchen floor, 10-year-old Jane watched her sadist father violated her mother till she breathed her last.

"What!" Joe exclaimed. "How could he do that to your mum, and in your presence? Damn!" He struck the pillow on the bed hard before tossing it aside. "I really want to see him right now and give him the beating of his life. It's no wonder you've been so bitter." He drew Jane into his embrace.

"I am so sorry for your pain, darling," he touched her face, and kissed her tears. "I promise to help you forget your pain."

Jane flashed a smile. "I understand, and I want to see my dad."

"What! That monster? Why?"

"Because I want to forget the past."

"Are you sure about this?" He searched her face. "Alright, if that is what you want. I will take you to him when we leave here."

Joe and Jane Allen went to see Desmond Harply at the maximum prison two days after the hospital discharged Jane. Jane and her father had an emotional reunion. Seeing Jane after such a long time, Desmond couldn't help but break down. He blamed himself for all the woes in their lives. Jane forgave Desmond for his inhuman actions towards her mother, even though he believed he didn't deserve it.

She urged him to surrender his life to Christ for peace. Desmond and Jane embraced, tears streaming down their faces as they mourned their pain. The prison supervisor informed Jane that her father has limited time left owing to terminal blood cancer, and Desmond declined further treatment. After Jane and Joe visited her father, Desmond Harply passed away, and their church members gathered to bury him.

***

Linda Allen asked Joe and Jane to come closer so she could better care for Jane. Regardless of Jane's claim of being in good health, Linda made it a priority to check on her every two days, and Jane eagerly embraced the attention. Jane wondered why she had been shying away from love all this while and put herself through undue heartaches.

A month after Jane's father died, Joe bought a mansion on ten acres of land. Jane had wanted to have a farm of her own and Joe made her dream come true. He bought her two horses and five goats with sixteen hens and two turkeys. Jane planned on opening a bigger chamber intending to go fully into real estate law and Joe fully gave her his support. Joe was glad he found her at last, and he planned on making all their time worthwhile.

Jane joined the chorister at Joe's family church, and she seemed to have developed a sense of humor out of the blue and more friendly. On a Saturday afternoon, Jane shared her good news with Joe.

"I have something to tell you, love."

With a quizzical look, which Joe eyed the envelope Jane had given him.

"Open it," Jane urged him.

Joe opened it, read the letterhead. He became tense upon discovering it was a hospital report. "Are you sick?"

"Read it, Joe," Jane ordered him with a straight face.

Joe read the report, trying to understand what he had just read. He left out a shout, "Lord!" Joe ran to Jane and lifted her up. "You are pregnant, Jane!" He wanted to be sure, but Jane simply nodded, overwhelmed with emotion.

After seventeen years and four months of marriage, Joe and Jane became parents to twin boys at 2:14am on a Thursday morning, with their friends and family by their side. Jane motioned for Joe to come closer as they watched their babies cry and the nurse clean them up, with the doctor smiling nearby. Both shared a simple prayer for their bundles of joy.

Jane looked up and whispered. "Thank you."

Joe understood her and will be eternally grateful for the joy he found in his family, the love they shared and for the ultimate love they both received. Under the doctor's gaze and amidst the cries of their babies, Joe's lips met Jane's, and they became lost in each other's embrace.

ABOUT THE AUTHOR

Bimpe Gold-Idowu began her literary journey as a young reader, devouring her older sister's books. She became obsessed with books and her imagination started developing characters. Bimpe's clean romance revolves around a confident woman protagonist and the theme of second chances in love. She co-author her science fiction books with her teenager first son, Richard O. Idowu. Bimpe, in addition, writes religious books about her experiences as a pastor.

Bimpe enjoys receiving feedback from readers, so please leave your honest review once you finish reading this story.

To get notified about my upcoming release, follow me on Amazon. Love you, and thanks for picking my book.

Website: www.bimpegoldidowu.com

Facebook: Bimpe Gold-Idowu

Twitter @gold_bimpe

Goodreeds Bimpe Gold-Idowu

Instagram: @bookkindle_bimpegoldidowu

Email: talktome@bimpegoldidowu.com, bimpegoldidowu@gmail.com

Linktree: linktr.ee/bimpegoldidowu

Tiktok: @bimpegoldidowubooks

SCAN THIS BARCODE TO ACCESS MY BOOKS AND SOCIAL HANDLES

BOOKS BY BIMPE GOLD-IDOWU

Overcoming Deceit: Expository on the World of Lies and Illusions

Overcoming Deceit explains lies the devil and deceitful people use in luring believers to their ways. When you are ignorant of deceitful ways, you will trust people without question, and this will either make you backslide or lose your focus.You may receive what we believe to be a better plan, or a shortcut to success. A new vision may come up, and you forget your true vision. Bimpe brings out several ways deceit may seem like truth to us. She exposed different ways the devil uses, and provide solutions on how to overcome each lie and illusion.

When Love Comes Calling: The Ultimate Love (Opposite Attraction Contemporary Romance)

Jane Harply is a successful woman haunted by her mother's death, and she has no love for the church. But when she falls for struggling film director Joe Allen, she realizes there's more to life than her past pain. They were happily married for a decade, but everything changes when Joe answers a higher calling and becomes a man of the cloth. Their separation is heart-wrenching, but Jane's world crumbles when she's diagnosed with a life-threatening heart condition.

Will Joe's faith and love bring them back together, or is it too late for a happily ever after?

Bimpe Gold-Idowu's powerful story of faith and love is a testament to the things that can be conquered when two hearts are intertwined.

The Adamite: Protector of the Universe on Kindle Vella

A failed coup by a dark archangel has set in motion a chain of events that will threaten the very existence of humanity. Five unsuspecting teenagers now hold the fate of the universe in their hands. When their science teacher, an archangel sent to stop the dark forces from destroying mankind, reveals a hidden secret, they are granted supernatural powers and tasked with protecting the Adam races from the incoming invasion. As the forces of darkness close in, the stakes get higher, and our heroes must come together to save the day. But will they be enough to stand up against the might of Zophra and his minions?

Join Bimpe Gold-Idowu on an epic journey through the universe that will leave you breathless. The Adamites is the first in an unmissable series that will leave you wanting more.

BIMPE BOOKS ON KINDLE VELLA: AN EPISODIC PLATFORM

This story takes us back to the beginning in the Phoenix Kingdom to reveal the rebelliousness of Zophra and his hatred towards a loyal angel. After Zophra escaped from the Cage of Hades in the upper court and came to planet earth, the loyal angel reincarnated as a human on planet earth as Jake Spielberg, but he couldn't remember his previous life. Betrayed his own teammate, would he be strong enough to defeat Zophra on his own or give up? Find out in the Alpha.

MY HEART
PREVAILS

BIMPE GOLD-IDOWU

Naomi Shander was the daughter of a multimillionaire and the only heir to the family fortune. She uncover the plot of her husband to be on her wedding day and was left heartbroken. Determined to start afresh, Naomi left her family in search of love in an unknown place where she met Jake Ericson, a widower and a man with the accusation of his wife's murder hanging over his head. Could Naomi love such a man?

THE HEART
MISSED
BIMPE GOLD-IDOWU

In 1892, the Idoro virus wiped an entire village out, it infiltrated the bloodstream, stopped the heartbeat and dried it up within six weeks. Sixty-eight years after, the village, filled with new residents, experienced another pandemic of the dreadful virus. The new villagers had to turn to Papa Harry for help, being the only survivor in the past, and he told them where to get the cure; a journey to Blue Cloudy Island, a place full of mysterious creatures. How would they survive on this island?